# CORRUPTED VESSELS

## and
# NEW EDEN

by Briar Ripley Page

tRaum Books
Munich, 2023

This is a work of fiction. No part of this book may be copied or redistributed without express permission from the author.

Cover art by Rysz Merey.

# Table of Contents

**Corrupted Vessels**..............................................6
    Part One.............................................7
    Part Two...........................................68

**New Eden**.......................................................140

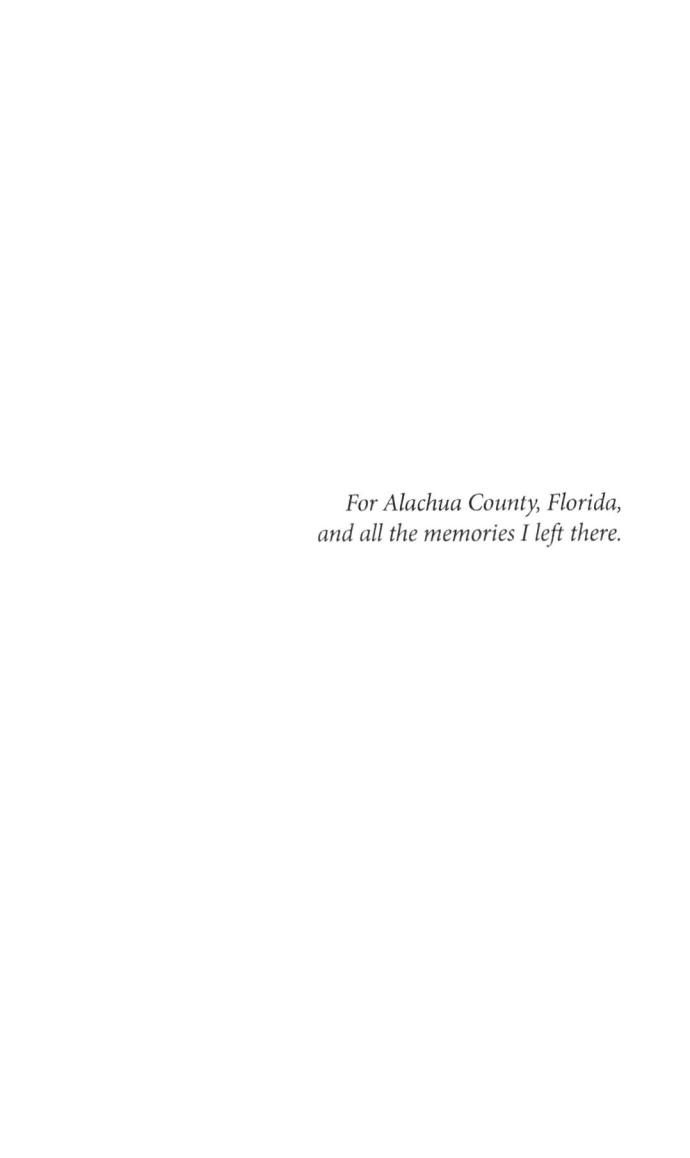

*For Alachua County, Florida,
and all the memories I left there.*

# Corrupted Vessels

**PART ONE**

The heart is deceitful
above all things

# I.

River watched Ash dance around the shadowy squat. He fiddled with the old Instamatic camera he'd stolen from his parents' attic before he had left their home forever. Ash's auburn curls swung in the opposite direction from their hands as they swayed and made slow, mystical gestures through the dusty air. It was late winter in the deep South, so the weather was pleasantly cool, the humidity bearable. River tried not to wonder how the two would fare without air conditioning once summer came creeping in with its clinging, sticky, fry-an-egg heat.

Ash would take care of everything, River assured himself. They'd said so. They'd promised. And they always had so far. Ash was special, a prophet. The silver and quartz rings on their fingers, charged like mystical batteries with moonlight and salt water instead of electric current, flashed beneath glints of green light. The light leaked through cracks in the inexpertly boarded-up windows of the abandoned house's second floor. Ash was humming. Then Ash was mumbling words that sounded like nonsense to River, but that he knew were really an angelic language.

Yes, it had seemed crazy at first. Apart from speaking to angels though, Ash didn't act like a crazy person. They were smarter than anyone else River had ever met. They could talk to all sorts of people, blending in easily among groups of men or groups of women; groups of dive bar pool players or gay nightclub ravers or upscale coffee house yuppies. Ash would simply adjust their posture and voice, take some jewelry off or put some on, and they would immediately be accepted into the fold. River, Ash's opposite, a perpetual outsider, had to skulk around the outskirts of the room until Ash returned to him triumphant, bearing a wad of cash or several scribbled-down phone numbers or an offer of food and a couch to crash on for the night. Ash had kept them both safe, sheltered, fed, and clothed for months of homeless wandering. Neither had gotten sick or badly injured, no one had attacked them or stolen from them, and the cops hadn't bothered them even once in all that time.

River remembered how much worse it had been for him before he had joined up with Ash. The only explanation for this kind of luck was genius, or magic. And if Ash, the genius, told River it was magic, who was he to argue?

River propped his bare, muddy feet up on the side of the doorframe. The peeling paint felt scratchy beneath his toes, and he scooted his back more firmly into the small, overturned table he was leaning against. The house was a mess now, but River was sure he and Ash would be able to fix it up into a home—and a temple, the way Ash wanted, of course. In any case, a place where they could both live for a pretty long time.

In the next room, Ash traced planetary symbols into the dirt and dust on the floorboards with the toes of their boots.

River decided to take a photo. He didn't use the camera much, but this seemed a worthy occasion to commemorate. Ash was deep in their ritual trance, paying no attention to River's activities, so it was probably safe. He lifted the camera, focusing on Ash, but making sure his grubby sweatpants and grubbier feet were in the frame too. This picture would be about the two of them together.

*Click. Flash.*

The Instamatic barfed out a snapshot; a blank gray square in the middle of a shiny white frame. River held it close to his face and watched the image form in slow patches. It looked good in the end, although his feet were washed-out blurs. Ash was a ghost in the background, their long copper hair and one pale hand the most visible parts of them. That was fitting, River thought, and he stuck the photo inside his Book for safekeeping. It nestled snug between his favorite pages, the ones with the black-and-white printed William Blake drawings that Ash had colored in with pencils. Ash had also given the drawings new titles, their photocopied handwriting sharper and blacker than the lines comprising the photocopied images. The picture of the beautiful, naked young man floating in a sphere filled with other nude figures was colored in shades of green and blue and gray, and Ash's swirling letters underneath it read, "RIVER ASSUMES HIS TRUE FORM IN THE FINAL DAYS." River, who did not look much like the beautiful, naked young man in the drawing at all and did not really believe he ever would, was touched almost to tears.

"Are you contemplating the world to come, kid?" Ash's lilting voice jolted River, made him bump his head against the table. He hadn't noticed his friend stop their ritual and cross the floorboards to stand beside him. It always amazed River how Ash could move without sound like that, even on old, uneven wood floors, in big, clompy boots. He looked up at Ash and tried not to sound awed, or spooked.

"I'm not a *child*," said River. "I'm nearly sixteen. That's, what, seven years younger than you?"

"Oh, more like seven *thousand*," said Ash. "Your soul is old, little River, but mine is far older. You'll always be a child to me." They chuckled.

River felt a surge of frustration. It was not a new frustration; it had been with him since he had first met Ash.

Ash bent gracefully and plucked River's photograph out of the Book. A tendril of their hair tickled River's cheek.

"What's this?" they asked. "A picture of me? River, you know you're not to take pictures of me. Or of *yourself*, for that matter." Their voice was light, but River knew what was coming. Still, he tried to plead his case.

"I would never use it against you, Ash. You know I wouldn't. I would never even show it to another person. This is just for me, just so I'll have something to remember today. It's special, and I want it to stay clear in my mind forever."

"I believe that you believe that," Ash said. "But you deceive yourself as to your true motives, River. You don't just want the memory, you want a piece of me. You want to control me and control my power. I can see that possessiveness in you, swirling through your aura like a dark fungal stain."

River felt his face burn. Of course Ash knew what he was thinking, knew his frustration at his age, his inexperience, the wrongness of his body, his recurring doubts, knew his jealousy of Ash's grace and sureness. He could never hide anything from them, or pretend to nobler feelings than what he had.

"I'm sorry," River whispered.

"That's all right," Ash assured him, tousling his lank,

greasy hair as though it wasn't disgusting at all. "I'll help you purify that stain. Let go of that possessiveness. You know what we have to do, don't you?"

"Yes," said River. He swallowed. "But it's a pretty long way back to the nearest body of running water, that creek near the highway—"

"No, no," Ash clucked. "Water is *your* primary element. For a photograph of *me*, we must perform a fire purification."

"My feet are in it," River pointed out.

"Faces and hands," said Ash with authority, "contain more of a body's spiritual essence than feet. Do you have a lighter, River?"

"I have a few. Most of them work, I think."

"Fetch me one that's yellow, or red."

River stood and pulled his army surplus jacket from behind the other side of the table. He rummaged through its pockets until he found a miniature neon orange Bic lighter. "Will this work?"

Ash nodded. "Acceptable. I'll begin preparing the ceremonial space in the front yard." They shook their head, rosy lips quirking in a rueful smile. "I had hoped we'd get the house a little more cleaned up this afternoon, but this—" they brandished the photograph at River, "is much too dangerous to leave for later."

River could sense the wretchedness accumulating around him like a fog. He could almost feel the clammy touch of that fungal stain only Ash could see. "I'm sorry," he said again.

"Don't apologize," said Ash. Their tone of voice that made it clear they were long suffering, but magnanimous enough not to hold River's fuck-ups against him.

"It's all right. What sort of spiritual guide would I be if I didn't help other fleshly pieces of God achieve enlightenment? If I didn't protect them from themselves and model correct behavior?"

River cracked his toes in the dust and dirt on the floorboards. They hurt, and left big ugly smudges like wounds. "Thank you, Ash," he said, sincerely.

Ash made a small fire outside the house and burned some fish skin they'd been keeping in their fanny pack (which allowed River to identify the source of a particular unpleasant smell that had been bugging him for days), some pine branches carved with angel-letters (which looked like aimless squiggles and spirals to River), and River's photograph (which melted from the edges, devouring Ash's ghost and River's feet lick by lick of greedy flame and oily black film). It was not a complicated ritual, but it took some time, particularly the branch carving. Ash did most of the work, but River knew he had to witness the whole thing, standing attentively by Ash's side without touching them. He focused until his eyes watered, even when Ash mumbled in the incomprehensible angel language for minutes on end. He kept his face a mask of reverence, even when Ash produced those wobbly, rotting shreds of fish skin and the smell made River gag. Ash would know if River's mind wandered; if he became bored or impatient or irritated. Ash always knew.

River wished that he understood the world the way Ash understood it. Barring that, he wished he could always approach their rituals with the awe he knew they deserved. But he couldn't, not any more than he'd been able to absorb the pastor's booming sin-and-damnation oratory when his parents had dragged him to church as a child. Of course, the pastor had probably been full of shit and Ash was probably right about everything. River no longer cared about his secret irreverence towards Jesus and Satan, but his conscience still spasmed with guilt that he had to work as hard as he did to look and behave in a spiritually acceptable manner for Ash.

Finally, as stars began to wink in an indigo sky and the song of night insects became oppressively loud, the photo and the fish skin and most of the branches were nothing but a smoldering rubble of sticky black stuff, charcoal, and ash.

"My holy namesake," said the prophet, and they thrust their hands into the mess, rings and all. More proof that Ash was no ordinary person: their flesh never burned. They used the soot to paint dark swirls across their pale cheeks, chin, and forehead. They drew lines between their freckles as though the flecks of pigment formed a map of constellations. Turned smiling to River and opened their arms wide. He rushed gratefully into his friend's embrace, savoring the softness of their cotton T-shirt and of their small, unbound breasts beneath it, the slight, hard curve of their stomach, the wiry muscle threaded through their whole body. He didn't mind the filthy handprints they left on his neck and back, the sooty dandruff in his hair.

"It's finished," Ash sighed. "All my power is fully returned to me. You saw the angel in the fire, didn't you, River?"

River thought about it. He remembered sharp spears of gold and orange, a low red and blue guttering, embers. No faces apart from Ash's face in the dissolving snapshot.

"I don't think so," he said.

"Well. You are still learning. I saw the angel. A heralding angel, a messenger of momentous change. It looked at me through the curtain of flame, with a mouth of ash and burning-cinder eyes, and it spoke into my mind." Ash paused dramatically. River, dutiful and curious, leaned in closer to Ash's chest, their beating heart.

"What did the angel say? Tell me."

"We're going to meet someone new soon, River. Maybe this week, maybe even tomorrow. Someone very important to both of us: another of the chosen fleshly gods. Whether of air or of earth, I do not know."

The bottom dropped out of River's belly. He was, suddenly, furious and terrified at the idea of having to share Ash with anyone else. Ash had spoken of finding the other two lost, amnesiac elemental deities trapped in human form ever since River had known them—ever since they'd met in the Asheville public library, back when River was still calling himself Jack. Still looking for some point to his existence or some road out of it. But River hadn't thought that they would find the vessel of air or the vessel of earth any time soon. He hadn't wanted them to, he was so happy with Ash alone. Fire and water, flowing through the fallen world together. He no longer needed an escape.

"Do... do you know anything else about the new person?" River mumbled. He clutched Ash to him, his fingernails digging into Ash's back beneath their thin shirt.

"Ow," Ash said. "Not so tight. You're scratching me. No, I don't know anything. Gender, age, appearance—*it could be anybody*. We must be especially attentive to strangers in the days to come."

"Mmm-hmmm," said River. "And then we'll only have one more to go?"

"Then we'll only have one more to go, and the final days will be upon us."

"Ash?" River swallowed. He listened to the rustling of invisible animals in the bushes all around them. *I'm not sure I want the final days to be upon us*, he thought. Aloud, he said, "It's dark. It'll be chilly soon. We should go inside and get our sleeping stuff out."

"Certainly," said Ash, pushing River gently away and smiling. "Certainly. It's your bedtime, little boy."

II. Linden sang as they walked through the sun-streaked forest, reveling in the warbling croak of their new voice. When they'd first started testosterone injections, they'd scrutinized themself daily, hourly, obsessively. Now, nine months later, they were more focused on other things, and the changes had snuck up on them. Weeks passed, and suddenly, they realized that they were getting called "sir" on the phone as often as "ma'am." That their friends were all making comments about how deep their voice sounded. When they recorded a new answering machine message for their phone and played it back, they barely recognized themself. For the first time in twenty-one years, Linden hadn't cringed at the sound of their own speech.

Now they hurled words and a rough approximation of melody at the live oaks and green light all around them, startling lizards and turtles, shaking the leaves, not caring that, objectively, they sounded terrible.

"No pixie, slut, or doxy shall take my Mad Tom from me!" Linden cheerfully picked their nose—no one was around to see. "I'll dance all night and with stars fight, but the fray, it shall become me!" Their voice soared and careened off rough bark and mossy stones. As they started in on the chorus, it echoed back to them:

"Yeah, it's well I sing, bonny boys *(...boys)*, bonny mad boys *(...mad boys)*, Bedlam boys are bonny *(...bonny)*..."

Linden paused. They stopped walking and stood on the narrow dirt path. The echo didn't sound like Linden's voice at all—it was high and sweet and fluid, almost the voice of a child. A choirboy voice. And it continued after Linden had stopped singing, in a faint honeyed chime:

"For they all go bare and they live by the air, and they want no drink nor money!"

Linden turned around slowly. A woodpecker drilled a nearby tree trunk. Something fluttered elsewhere in the canopy. They could, just barely, hear the rumble of cars on the nearest road. But who was singing? Where was the voice coming from? Linden considered themself a rational sort of person, and they were not easily spooked. There was something eerie about the bodiless voice though, something that raised the small hairs on Linden's forearms and at the back of their neck. Linden tried not to imagine a lurking, whispering spirit—some pale-skinned demonic little kid out of a horror movie. *Stupid*, they thought to themself. *It's three p.m. on a Wednesday, and you're cutting through a patch of undeveloped woods in your big college town on your way home from art history class. Also, malevolent ghost children aren't real.*

After a moment of tense, rustling voicelessness, the singing came again, repeating the chorus of the song. Linden realized that their perception had been off. They had thought they were hearing a soft, faint voice very near them, instead, the singer was loud and farther away. Somewhere off the path, beyond the thick bushes, trees, and long grass. Linden's curiosity was piqued. Who was wandering around out there? They never saw other people when they took this shortcut, though the cleared pathway implied someone's presence.

Linden looked around the path once more in the peaceful, shimmering leaflight. They had plenty of time before sunset. It was pleasantly cool, but not chilly. Linden didn't have plans until much later that evening. Everything was well-aligned for a little expedition, they decided. Linden carefully tucked the ends of their jeans into their socks—the woods were full of ticks—and stepped off the path, in the direction from which they thought the voice had come. They did not sing now. They walked softly from toe to heel, like their cousin who'd been a Boy Scout had taught them. The long grasses and thorny weeds rustled around their thighs as they pushed farther and farther into the wilderness. An osprey watched Linden fiercely from a high branch, ruffling its neck feathers. The sound of the woodpecker faded, but the sound of the singing grew louder and stronger.

*This kid is really belting it,* thought Linden. *Whoever he is, he's got a future in musical theater. Or at least in regional Ren Faire performances.*

A shape rose out of the Spanish-moss drapery and tree-trunk Venetian blinds like a Magic Eye puzzle. At first, Linden caught only glimpses of it in the spaces between other things, and they weren't sure they were seeing it right. There couldn't be a house out here, could there? These woods surely weren't so big that they could hide a whole two-story house nobody knew about. Maybe Linden had gotten turned around somehow, was coming out of the forest's edge without realizing it, and they were looking at the peaked roof and gingerbread trim of an ordinary old house in the suburbs. Maybe it was a trick of the light and the landscape had made the house appear to be standing in the middle of the woods, surrounded by wildflowers, long grass, and twisted thickets of bush and vine. Linden took a step forward in the direction of the apparent house, and then another.

Knees high and stride long to avoid fallen logs and big rocks.

"I went to Pluto's kitchen to break my fast one morning! And there I got souls piping hot that on a spit were turning!" sang the voice.

Linden broke through the trees and into a clearing. There was indeed a two story house sitting by itself in the middle of the woods. It was dilapidated, with some windows boarded up or broken, a roof shedding shingles, and paint that might once have been white but was now a mottled yellow specked with the greens, browns, and blacks of mold and fungus. It peeled away from the gingerbread trim, the windowsills, and the front door like old bandages. Linden could tell at a glance that no one had lived in the house for a long, long time.

...Except maybe someone *had*, because the source of the voice was standing casually on the sagging front porch, back leaned up against the mouldering side of the house like they belonged there.

The voice didn't belong to a choirboy after all, Linden saw, but to a young woman in her mid-to-late teens. She was short and chubby and rather plain, with sunburned arms and a limp brunette mullet. The girl wore a long gray-green dress, which either didn't fit her or was entirely shapeless by design. The hem touched her bare toes and was dirty. Silver threads winked in the dress's thin fabric. Linden began to wade through milkweed and jessamine, not bothering with stealth any longer. The house's occupant didn't look dangerous. Either she'd welcome Linden, or she'd tell them to fuck off and that would be that.

"Hey!" called Linden as they approached. "Hi there!

I heard you singing—you have a beautiful voice—and I wondered if..."

The young woman's dark eyes went wide. They were already large, and now, they seemed to take up most of her face. Her small, bucktoothed mouth gaped, but she said nothing. Her song had dried up in her throat. Before Linden had reached the edge of the porch steps, before they had time to finish their sentence, the young woman scuttled to the front door, wrenched it open, disappeared into its dim maw, and slammed it shut with a dusty thud. Linden thought they could hear the faint tread of footsteps clambering up a staircase.

This reaction was strange and unexpected. Still, there was no hurt in knocking at the door once or twice before they started back home, was there? Maybe the young woman was just extremely shy.

The rotting porch steps squelched and creaked beneath Linden's high tops. The house's paint looked even shabbier close up. The doorknob was a scab of rust. Linden took a deep breath, made a fist with their right hand, and rapped once, sharp and deliberate, in a spot relatively free of decay. The sound wasn't very loud, but the door swung open immediately. Linden jumped back in surprise.

The person standing in the doorway was not the young woman who had been singing before. Linden could not guess either the person's gender or their assigned sex. (They felt a flash of guilt for trying, then a flash of jealousy. Why couldn't Linden be so perfectly androgynous?) The person simply Was, like a work of art or a force of nature. A forest spirit.

They were a head taller than Linden, who wasn't

short. Long-limbed and thin the way rock stars are thin: the body of a young Patti Smith or David Bowie. Bright auburn curls spilled thick and loose to the person's collarbones. Their nose, chin, and cheekbones were stark beneath milky skin dusted with freckles. Their broad eyebrows seemed to have a natural arch. Their eyes were a very light blue, like a sled dog's, and the color gave an eerily vacant impression for a moment before the person's lips broke into a sunny smile, revealing a chipped incisor and dimples in both cheeks.

"Welcome," they breathed. "Welcome, welcome, dearest friend."

Their voice was as heady, appealing, and ambiguous as their face. Smiling and glowing, they brushed a lock of hair behind a small, perfect shell of an ear. Linden saw that their long fingers were covered in what looked like hippie junk jewelry, the kind of silver-plated rings set with polished ovals of quartz or glass that Linden's spaciest aunt favored. On Linden's aunt, they were slightly embarrassing—on this person, they were romantic, iconoclastic, gorgeous in the golden afternoon. The rings glittered. The stranger glittered. Linden stared and felt their clit swell in their boxers. Felt the place just behind it twinge and throb. They took a large step backwards on the porch and shook their head rapidly to clear it. *Stop thinking with your groin.*

"Friend?" Linden asked the stranger. "Excuse me, but I don't think we've ever met before. I'm Linden. I'm a student at the university, and I just happened upon your house here..."

"*Linden!*" exclaimed the stranger, interrupting. "Of course, of course. The vessel of earth. And you've your name already. How perfect. The angel spoke true."

Linden cleared their throat. They didn't like to think that the beautiful stranger was crazy, but the beautiful stranger certainly *sounded* crazy. Probably they were just high, or excited. Linden could still get the conversation on track, make friends. Linden suddenly wanted nothing more in the world than to be friends with this person. (Well. More than *friends*.)

"Glad you like the name. I picked it myself. What's yours?"

"I'm Ash, the vessel of fire and the chosen prophet of the world to come. And this is River, the vessel of water." Ash gestured behind them, and Linden realized that the singer was there too, lurking nervously in the shadows at the foot of the stairs to the house's second floor. She was hunched over on the bottom step, picking at loose threads in the skirt of her dress.

"Oh, yeah." Linden decided to ignore the "vessel" nonsense for now. Probably these people were Wiccans or something. A little cringey, but hey, who was Linden to judge? "I heard her singing, before. Outside. That's how I found you guys. Actually, I wanted to tell her how good her voice is. How much I liked it." Linden attempted a smile at the dour lump swathed in gloom and loose fabric.

"'Her'?" A minute furrow emerged between Ash's magnificent eyebrows. "River is a boy."

River looked up and glared at Linden. "I'm a boy," he confirmed, and then, slowly, almost mockingly, "I use he/him pronouns. I identify as male. *You* get it, I'm sure."

Linden was mortified. Of course, they—of all people!—should have known better than to assume. Then again, he was wearing a dress... but wasn't it just as essentialist to judge a person's gender based on his clothes as on his physiology? And now that Linden looked away from Ash's hypnotic face and hands, they saw that Ash wore a dress, too. It was nearly identical to River's, but made of a bright red fabric that had the cheap not-silk sheen of a drugstore Halloween costume. The hem ended several inches above Ash's feet, which were shod in a pair of heavy, utilitarian black boots.

"I use they/them!" Linden blurted out, attempting to negate their embarrassment, and River's, and maybe even Ash's. As soon as they had, they wished they could take it back. River looked even more hostile than before.

"Good for you," he said. This time, there was unmistakable venom in his tone.

But Ash clapped their hands together like a child, and their smile returned. "So do I!" they exclaimed, as though it was an incredible coincidence. "We are all of us neither one thing nor the other in this house. Please, come in. Stay for tea."

Tea? Linden wondered, as Ash moved aside to allow them through the doorway. The interior of the house was almost as decrepit as its exterior, although someone had made an effort to clear the floor and stairs of dust, dirt, and debris. Tattered wallpaper drooped over a banister that cracked and splintered in the middle. Shelves of fungus erupted from the back of an armchair. Linden saw a cockroach scuttle around River's filthy toes. There was no light in the house but that which came through the windows, and Linden found it almost impossible to believe that Ash and River had plumbing here, or a stove, or a functioning kitchen, or any of the requirements for tea preparation. Still, with Ash smiling at them, making steady eye contact, even reaching out to brush the back of Linden's hand with warm fingers, they would have agreed to go almost anywhere and do almost anything. River trailed behind Ash and Linden like a reluctant shadow as they walked to a back room on the first floor of the house.

The room clearly *had* been a kitchen once, based on the faucet and the stove, both coated in rust. There were plants growing wild in the sink. A darker patch on the sun-bleached floor might have marked a refrigerator's former location. Through a door-less door frame, the room just beyond the kitchen was visible too. There, light fell through a long, ornate stained glass window. The glass was abstract, all color and shape, no sense that Linden could see. Ash led Linden through the kitchen, past the plants and the possible refrigerator's ghost, into the kaleidoscope the window created on the walls and floor and ceiling.

"Sit down!" said Ash, in a voice both good-humored and commanding. They gestured at the empty, splintered floor. Linden hesitated for a moment, but once River stalked in and seated himself cross-legged amidst a bouquet of refracted blue lozenges and red triangles, Linden cautiously lowered their ass to the ground and sat with their knees bent in front of them. It wasn't comfortable. Ash retreated to the kitchen, clattered around for a thirty-second eternity, then returned to the kaleidoscope.

"Tea," Ash announced, placing cups and saucers on the floor in front of River and Linden. The cups and saucers were made of china as pale blue as Ash's eyes, rims painted gold. They were cracked, chipped, and dirty inside. River's had no handle. He picked it up and inspected it, then looked over at Linden with an unpleasant expression on his face. Ash sat down with their own cup and saucer—significantly less damaged, Linden noticed—and a half-empty liter bottle of...

"Diet Mountain Dew?" Linden asked.

"Well," said Ash, "I can't actually make us tea right now. This will have to do. But it's got caffeine in it, and it looks so pretty in the cups! Let's pretend, shall we?"

Ash poured the soda in each teacup—first their own, then Linden's, then River's. There was some kind of cheap liquor mixed in with it; the smell made the hairs inside Linden's nostrils curl when they caught a whiff. The yellowgreen liquid and the blue china did make a nice color together, but it wasn't a color Linden particularly wanted to drink. Specks of black stuff floated to the top of Linden's cup—meanwhile, Ash and River both sipped at theirs with evident enjoyment. Linden watched the specks swirl around in their yellow/green/blue Mountain Dew lake.

"It's wonderful tea, Ash," said River.

"Thank you, dear," said Ash.

Linden wondered if they were a couple. River seemed too young for the twenty-something Ash, but maybe he was just baby-faced.

"So," asked Linden, hoping the other two wouldn't notice that they weren't drinking, "how long have you guys lived in this house? What brings you here?"

"Providence and the road, to answer your second question," said Ash. "As to the first: about five, six days, I think. Time is elusive and illusory. It's so hard to keep track."

"It's been six days," said River. "We've finally got most of the floors pretty clean and all the really unusable junk moved out."

"Yes, the temple was quite a wreck when we first found it." Ash beamed, dazzling. "I suppose it wasn't even a temple then! Only a house, with the potential for holiness encircling it like a beacon. Angels showed me the way, through auras and signs."

"But you two are turning it into a temple?" Except for the stained glass window, the house didn't seem like any place of worship Linden had ever encountered. "For your, uh, *religion?*"

The tiny furrow appeared between Ash's eyebrows again, and their smile melted off. "It's already a temple," Ash said. "True, we haven't put up proper altars yet, but you ought to be able to tell anyway. *You* ought to." They ran a hand through their curls. "And *religion* is a name for humans' belief in what they cannot see or know. Faith, plus codified rites and rituals. We have rituals too, but they come directly from the angels all around us. Because the angels speak to me, there's no need for simple *faith.*"

Linden dismissed an impulse to apologize for their lack of insight into Ash's worldview. Charming as Ash was, this was ridiculous stuff.

"You're telling me that *angels* talk to you? Angels. Like, dead people in robes with long hair and harps and wings?"

"Angels aren't *dead people*," said River in the tone of someone forced to explain an obvious fact to an adult who ought to know better. "They're eternal. They were never born, and they can't die."

"Nor do they wear clothes," added Ash. "Unless those clothes are made of fire, or water, or earth, or air. Most of them don't look human at all." They sighed, and their smile half-returned for a brief moment. "You're even more confused than River was when I first found him. Then again, earth is the strongest classical element on the plane of mortal, earthly bodies. It would be easier for you to forget yourself in human form, and harder for you to embrace true Knowledge."

Linden could hear the capital K in Knowledge. They fought not to roll their eyes. "Listen," they said, "I've never been in the habit of just believing whatever crazy thing a stranger feels like telling me, and I don't intend to start now. Can we talk about something else? You seem fascinating. I'm sure you've both got lots of different interests." Their eyes cast about the room, looking for something anodyne to comment on. There was really only one thing there at all.

"How about that stained glass window, huh?"

"Ah, yes." Ash floated one be-ringed hand through a prismatic glimmer of light in the air. "The Auspicious Window. It's lovely, isn't it? But you'll see, it's one of the signs that we were all meant to come together in this place." They pointed at the collage of glass shapes. "Look. The green river for our River. The red and blue flames for me. The spears of amber for you. Those white clouds for the vessel of air, whenever he or they or she or it arrives."

Linden supposed they could see the elemental landscape Ash imagined in the window's pattern if they squinted a little. "What about those lavender bits?" they asked, humoring. "And the dark purple?"

"The angels that surround and connect us all," Ash replied, serene. They leaned so close to Linden that Linden could smell their breath, its boozy, improbable sweetness. Linden was so lost for words that they took a swig from their cup. The chemical citrus of the soda went poorly with the tongue-peeling sting of whatever alcohol had been mixed into it. There was a charcoal and dirt undercurrent to the whole affair that Linden refused to think too much about.

"You'll learn," said Ash. "You'll learn it all. I'll show you." Suddenly, they put their hand on Linden's thigh, almost at the place where Linden's leg joined to the hip, and tickled, and stroked, and *squeezed*. Linden's teacup fell from their hand, dousing their chest and belly in sticky, smelly drink the color of dehydrated piss. The cup clattered and rolled to the floor, but didn't break.

"*Fuck!*" They pushed themselves away from Ash, stood, and began backing towards the front door of the house. "Don't *do* that! Haven't you heard of goddamn consent? Boundaries?" Their shoes fumbled around warped wooden boards, then loose kitchen tiles.

River looked astonished.

Ash simply stared at Linden with those implacable blue eyes, that porcelain face, that faint, dimpled half-smile.

Linden felt an unwelcome flare of arousal lance through their anger. *No*, they thought fiercely in the direction of their cunt. They turned the corner, into the room with the fungus-encrusted armchair, and Ash and River disappeared. No voices or sounds followed Linden from the kitchen.

Still, Linden felt the need to shout a final few words

as they darted for the door and tumbled back into the afternoon woods.

"I'm not going to be part of your weird sex cult!"

Smoking wasn't allowed in the bar, but it always smelled overwhelmingly of smoke anyway. Linden sniffled and squinted as they hunched over their phone, absent-mindedly scrolling through the Wikipedia article on Classical Elements. It was pretty hokey stuff—Linden couldn't help thinking of the old Captain Planet cartoon. The webpage showed a diagram of supposed elemental spheres, dated 1617, with earth (Terra) a dull orb at the bottom, covered by a layer of water (Aqua), which was covered by air (Aer), which was covered by a topmost layer of fuzzy, wavering flames. Fire (Ignis).

"Linden!" Nora exclaimed, giving Linden a friendly shove in the shoulder. "What gives, dude? You haven't touched your beer!"

"Uh?" Linden put their phone down. "Sorry, I was distracted. A weird thing happened to me today, you know..."

"Oh my god," said Nora. "You have to tell me all about it—wait," she turned to another member of their group, Jamie, who was laughing much too loudly and having trouble balancing on his barstool, drunk already. "Jamie, honey, do you need help? Do you need some water?"

"I need another drink," Jamie slurred. "*Shotsh!*"

"Absolutely not," said Nora. "No shots. I can drive you back to the dorms, if you want."

"Ish not my *fault*, Noraaaa," groaned Jamie. He

pointed to the opposite corner of the bar, where a pretty magenta-haired woman in a crop top was flirting with a person who looked too young to drive, let alone drink, despite their mascara'd on mustache, bolo tie, and coxcomb mohawk. "Lookit that. Fuckin' Shophie. Abusive *bish*. 'Bout to get her claws into some poor lil' faggy bashterd. Can't stand to see it..."

"Hey." Nora thumped his back. "Your ex has as much right to be here as you do. Let's not use slurs, okay?" She glanced at the duo across the room. "That kid does look awfully young. I'll go talk to Sophie, make sure everything's above board. Linden, you mind watching Jamie for a sec? I think Nat and Mel are a little distracted." She jabbed a thumb at the other two friends they'd come to the bar with, who had migrated from their barstools to the jukebox by the unisex washroom and appeared to be deep in an argument.

"Sure," said Linden. Their desire to tell Nora about the afternoon's disturbing tea party, about River and Ash, was decreasing by the second. The world of the bar was so far removed from all that, so filled with petty, childish cruelties and tedious dramas barely held in check by the patience of Nora and others like her. Why bother Nora with more problems she'd feel obligated to sort through? And would Nora even understand someone like Ash? Linden didn't understand Ash, but they knew—they felt deep in their heart and gut and cunt—that Ash was special, for all their obvious insanity and their leg-grabbing. It's not like I didn't want them to touch me that way, thought Linden. I just wasn't expecting it. And in front of River...

Linden looked into the golden bubbling of their lager, but it reminded them too much of the teacups filled with rotgut Mountain Dew. They watched Jamie crying pathetically into his folded arms beside them, warbling about Sophie's treachery. They saw Nora speaking to Sophie, looking motherly and harried, while Sophie crossed her arms and smirked, and the kid she'd been hitting on sidled bashfully out the bar's side door and into the night.

Linden twisted around on the farting vinyl of their stool to watch Nat and Mel snipe at each other, waving tattooed arms and snarling with black lipsticked mouths. A tall person in a sparkling dress and a short one in a tuxedo print T-shirt were ignoring all the commotion and slow-dancing around the sticky linoleum floor together. They were an elegant pause in the midst of mundane sound and fury. The tall person had a wild head of cropped dark red curls that reminded Linden of Ash. Unlike Ash's hair, this person's was dyed.

The dancers swayed into each other's bodies. The short one brazenly lowered a hand from the small of the tall one's back, cupping and squeezing their ass through the slinky, spangled fabric of the short dress. The tall person returned the gesture in kind as the two turned in a slow circle, not caring who could see. *I see*, thought Linden, feeling drunk although they had barely had half a beer.

"Geez Louise." Nora returned to her stool. "Sophie's really going to land herself in trouble one of these days. Her and Jamie both—they've got to stop drinking so much." She shook her head and nudged Jamie in the shoulder. "Hey, Jamie. Let's go, okay? I'm beat, you're loaded... we should quit while we're ahead."

"Fuckin' *fine*," grumbled Jamie. "Okay. Lesh go." Nora helped him up, and he tumbled against her sturdy frame like a broken scarecrow.

"Linden?" Nora asked, looking softly at her friend. "You coming with us?" She gave Linden one of her slightly sad, secretive smiles. The little silver crescent in her nose piercing flashed as she shifted under the flickering, multicolored bar lights. Linden thought of slim fingers, covered in shiny rings.

"Yeah." Linden thrust their phone into the back pocket of their jeans. "I'm not feeling the bar tonight. Nat and Mel can find their own way home."

"Their apartment's in walking distance. Help me with Jamie, would you?" Nora took one of Jamie's arms, and Linden took the other. The three of them left the bar and lumbered like a many-limbed beast across the lightless parking lot. Nora's Civic waited patiently for them, dented in its passenger side door and smelling mostly of peach air freshener, although Nora did smoke cigarettes.

"So," Nora said, sounding half-interested, "what was it you were going to tell me? Something strange happened to you this afternoon?"

Nora and Linden had dropped Jamie off at his dorm, and Nora had seen that he got inside safely. Now they were slowly cruising towards the housing co-op where they both lived. Nora was more involved in the ideological aspects of cooperative housing; Linden liked having a room to themself for cheaper than they could get it anyplace else, and not having to cook most nights. It was, Linden imagined, a lot like living in an old-fashioned boarding house, albeit with a little more vegan food and a lot more punk shows in the basement.

"Oh, that." Linden glanced over at Nora. She kept her eyes on the road—Linden noticed the heavy bags beneath them. "It wasn't much. I was cutting home on that path through the woods, like I do, and I saw this falling-down old abandoned house out there. Not a little shack, but a real two-story house, kinda Victorian-looking. There was moss and mold growing all over the walls."

"Huh," said Nora. "Did you go inside?"

"No. I don't think there'd have been anything worth investigating."

"*Investigating*." Nora chuckled. "You sound like a private eye."

"No way." Linden watched bands of light and darkness streak across the ceiling of the car. "I'm going to be a reporter. Or maybe a novelist. Or a professional Twitch streamer."

"That's it, then? You saw an abandoned house in the woods?"

"Well, I mean... I don't *know*, Nora. I just thought it was weird. Where did it come from? How old is it? Why hasn't it been torn down? Why is it out there all by itself?"

"God only knows." Nora clicked her tongue. "It's not like our public infrastructure's great. Maybe the city can't afford to have it torn down, and nobody else cares if it rots out there. Hell, I think it's kinda cool if it rots out there. Going back to the soil."

"Very cool."

Companionable silence sat between the pair for six

blocks and change. It left the car with them after Nora parked in the gravel driveway behind Carl's van and Jamal's Camry. The silence walked up the front steps and through the door with them, past a common room where lots of people were still awake and talking, up the stairs. It paused with them on the first landing.

Linden lived in one of four rooms on the second floor; Nora had one half of the house's little attic. Nora spoke first.

"Linden," she said, touching her friend's shoulder and holding their gaze. She still looked tired, but she was smiling, and something avid and mischievous swam in her eyes. "It's been a little while. What do you say? Can I spend the night with you again?"

"Just as friends, right?" Linden asked. The day before, they would have hoped the answer might finally be... something other than what it always was. Now, their mind was full of Ash, the pleasurable itch of desire tangled in auburn curls and the sharp angles of thin white limbs. Ash, so different from round, solid Nora, with her golden-brown skin, her razor-straight black hair.

"Just as friends." She began to rub Linden's arm slowly, up and down. Linden thought of Ash's fingers on their thigh. They remembered the hard press of all those rings.

Linden leaned into Nora's fat belly and small, soft breasts, embracing her tightly. They kissed with open mouths and Linden ran their fingers through Nora's sensible bob while Nora moved her hand from Linden's arm to the back of their skull, rubbed the coarse, close-buzzed stubble there. Nora smelled like artificial peaches. She tasted vaguely of tobacco and tar.

"Let's go into my room," murmured Linden. They led Nora through the door, and she pulled them down onto Linden's unfolded futon couch-bed. Linden began to unbutton the row of fake pearl buttons on Nora's shirt. She put a hand down the back of Linden's jeans. They nibbled at each other's lips, and Linden wondered what Ash might taste like. Was Ash a smoker?

Kissing, touching, wet prod of fingers. Warm molten softness of tender skin on skin. Linden kept closing their eyes, imagining Ash rolling around on the futon with them, how different Ash would feel beneath their mouth and hands, how Ash's tongue might delicately lather their clit, their thighs. It felt unfaithful, wrong and perverse, despite Nora's frequent assertions that she didn't want a romantic relationship, didn't want monogamy right now. Linden tried to keep the thoughts out, to focus on being with Nora. Nora who was so sensible and sane, so responsible, so good at respecting people's boundaries and asking for consent. Nora, who Linden thought of as the most beautiful woman they knew.

It didn't work. Ash came back like the flame on a trick candle, their rings and dimples and burning blue eyes driving Linden on and on, deeper and deeper, until convulsive shudders ran through both lovers and Nora was making quiet, breathy sounds, as though she was in pain. She didn't seem to notice that anything was amiss, that Linden's mind was elsewhere. Ash's eyes were painted on the backs of Linden's eyelids, their hand a phantom between Linden's legs. Linden spasmed and quaked, biting their lip to keep from crying out and disturbing the rest of the house. They tasted blood. They kept going.

**III.** River thought he might hate Linden, and he hated himself for it, as they had never said a cruel word to him. They didn't even condescend to him the way Ash so often did. Linden bought River and Ash boxes of pads and tampons so they wouldn't have to shoplift those anymore, and wouldn't have to use quadruple-layered gas station paper towels that rubbed them raw. Linden brought them bottled water and sandwiches.

But River couldn't forget their first meeting, when Linden had assumed he was female.

Linden, not as tall as Ash but still taller than women usually were, with muscled arms, narrow hips, a downy black mustache, and a deep voice. They looked more like a man than River ever would, ever could, even if he got on T somehow, and Linden didn't even want to *be* a man. Not really, not the way *River* wanted to be a man. It wasn't fair. Linden had stood in the doorway, clean and well-fed and confident, with their broad shoulders and buzz cut, and they had looked at River crouched on the stairs and seen not just a kid, but a *girl*. Until that moment, River hadn't thought of the robe Ash had made for him (back in West Virginia, where they'd stayed for several days in a punk house that had a sewing machine) as at all dress-like. Afterwards, he couldn't see it as anything but a dress, even when Linden had agreed to don the earth robe Ash had sewn so many months before.

Since Ash had not known Linden when they had made it, the robe didn't fit right. It clung too tightly to Linden's torso and ended in the middle of their wolf-hairy shins instead of at their ankles. Still, on Linden, as on Ash, it looked mystical and devoid of gender, like something a druid might wear. River, neither blessed with access to testosterone, nor with fortunate genes, had to go around looking like a girl in a dress.

He couldn't change back into his regular clothes. Although Ash had never explicitly forbidden it, nor even ordered River to follow their lead when they'd started wearing the red robe all the time, River understood how disappointed Ash would be. How pathetic he'd seem compared to Linden, who spent more and more time at the house with them. Who grew ever larger and brighter in Ash's esteem.

Right now, Linden and Ash were out back of the house, discussing their plans to build a composting toilet. It was a Saturday, so Linden didn't have classes, didn't have homework due the next day, and would probably stay for a long time. Not overnight; Linden never stayed overnight, although they did fuck Ash in the upstairs bedroom at least four times a week. River wasn't sure if the two thought he couldn't hear them or if they just didn't care that he did.

*We don't need a composting toilet,* River thought sulkily. He was curled on the balding velvet cushion of the armchair in the living room, a blob of boy on its front to match the mass of fungus on its back. *I'm fine shitting in a hole in the dirt. Burying it like a cat. Pissing on top. Letting all my waste go straight back to the world with no in-between phase. Isn't that part of what being an embodied elemental deity is supposed to mean?* He knew he was being ridiculous, but he persevered on this line of thought for a few more minutes anyway. He played with his orange lighter, flicking it on and off, off and on, watching the flame hiss and jump, wondering what would happen if he lit the fungus, the chair.

River considered fetching his camera, which had been collecting dust in the second floor's ex-bathroom. Since the day after the incident where he'd tried to photograph Ash on the sly, River had turned the claw-foot tub into a nest for himself. How long had it been now? Nearly a month, he was pretty sure. He hadn't dared—even when he knew Ash was far away and otherwise occupied!—to take photographs of sunsets, inanimate objects, the Auspicious Window, his own feet and hands. Now, he fantasized about creeping out the back door, capturing a tiny Linden and a tiny Ash in a shiny white square. That would show them. He'd have something they didn't.

River clicked the lighter again and yelped when he accidentally singed his fingertips. He hurled the little piece of plastic across the room, where it bounced against a windowpane and dropped to the floor with a dull rattle.

He wouldn't take any snapshots, of course. Ash would find out, one way or another, and then Ash would stare at him with burning blue disappointment. He would lose another sliver of respect and trust. He'd lose another sliver of advantage over Linden, who had tried to use their phone to take pictures of Ash, River, and the house on their second visit. Ash had been livid, and the rest of the afternoon and evening was spent in elaborate triple-purification ceremonies. Ash had even wanted to destroy Linden's phone, suggesting they ought to immerse it in water, then burn it in a bonfire, and finally bury it beneath the ground. Linden had talked them down from this idea, but only by showing Ash that all the photos had been deleted and swearing up, down, and sideways that they'd never use their phone during a visit again. Ash had insisted that Linden get on their knees in front of Ash, and then in front of River, and promise.

River smiled at the memory.

The door squealed open and a warm breeze blew through the house. River recognized Linden's footsteps—heavier and less intentional than Ash's—a moment before he heard their croaky voice.

"Man, River, are you sitting in that gross chair again? You guys don't have to have moldy furniture, y'know. I could fix you up with something from Goodwill." Linden loped across the living room, sweat shining in the hair on their upper lip and on their wide, olive forehead. They lifted the orange lighter from where it lay and brought it back to River, resting flat in the middle of their upturned palm like a gift from royalty.

River snatched it away and stuck it in the pocket of his jacket, which he'd taken to wearing on top of his robe at all times, even though it was usually too hot for it.

"Thanks," he said, sounding bitter and sarcastic even to himself. He cursed internally. *Goddamn it, can't you even try to be friendly?*

"Ash is peeing," said Linden. "Don't worry, soon we'll have built that toilet. While they're out... River, can I talk to you?"

"You're already talking to me." River hunched into the jacket and pulled its sleeves over his hands.

"Sure, sure," Linden's smile seemed forced. "Listen, about these robes... do you think I could persuade Ash to let me take them home and wash them? They're starting to get disgusting. Just, rank as hell. No offense." They trailed their hand along the faded, nubbly brown-and-tan flannel of their robe. "I'd at least like to wash mine. This fabric's kind of heavy, and the weather's warming up. Look, I've got pit stains." They raised one arm to demonstrate. River wrinkled his nose.

"If we were supposed to wash the robes, I could do it in a service station bathroom. Or I'd use some of the money we've saved to get a machine at a laundromat. We know how to keep ourselves clean, Linden."

"I'm sorry! I only meant—"

"You *know* Ash doesn't want them washed," said River, trying for a tone both reproachful and righteous. "You were there when Ash said so."

"Yeah, but they never explained *why*, and I think—"

"Are you questioning Ash?" River glared at Linden as fiercely as he could. It wasn't like he had never questioned Ash's choices or Ash's wisdom before. But he knew enough to feel ashamed when he did, and besides... Linden questioning Ash felt different. Linden was a newcomer. Linden hadn't been with River and Ash when they were hitchhiking, hopping trains, on the streets. Linden had perfect teeth and literary analysis papers to write. They were always so fucking confident, walking around like they knew everything. Like they knew more than Ash, who spoke with angels.

"Yes, River," Linden blinked, seeming surprised or amused or who cared what emotion, really. "Yes, I'm questioning Ash. I mean," their voice dipped conspiratorially, "you don't... *believe* in all of Ash's angel, elemental, end of the world stuff, do you?"

"Of course I do!" River was aghast. "So do you! You have to—you're the vessel of earth. Why else would you come back here? Why else..." he trailed off, remembering the slapping and squelching and snuffling and moaning that poured through the wall between the upstairs bedroom and his bathtub bed at night. The vast dilation of Linden's pupils whenever Ash smiled at them, or otherwise expressed approval.

"Ash is an amazing person," said Linden. "Truly. And I don't mind playing along with this stuff most of the time. It might not be the healthiest thing for Ash, but I'm no psychologist—it's not my place to judge. They seem to have done a good job keeping themself safe and keeping you safe. But no, I don't believe in literal angels, and I don't believe I'm anything more special than a normal human being, and I don't believe that taking pictures of people traps their souls, or whatever. It's a really interesting, beautiful story. That's all that it is. And I want to wash these robes, no matter what Ash's compulsions say. They're probably crawling with bacteria."

"I'll tell Ash," hissed River. "I'll tell Ash you said that. They'll be upset. Maybe they'll throw you out. Maybe you were a *mistake*. Maybe the angels were *wrong*."

"No, wait—" Linden looked worried.

The door opened again and Ash drifted into the house.

"Ash!" River cried out. He noted Linden's trembling lower lip with pleasure. "Guess what Linden just told me?"

Ash came over to stand beside the chair. They looped an arm around Linden's waist. "Something very astute, I'm sure," Ash said, gazing affectionately at their lover. Linden was staring at River. They mouthed a word at him that might have been "Don't" or "No" or "Please."

"Linden wants us to wash our robes," said River.

"Linden says they don't understand why we can't wash them. Linden," he finished in scandalized tones, "thinks they smell bad. Linden called them *disgusting*."

Ash frowned and removed their arm from Linden. They took a step backward and planted their hands on their sparkling red hips.

"Did they."

"They did," River confirmed. "I said you knew best, of course."

"The angels know best," Ash corrected. They heaved a disappointed, angry sigh. "I would have thought you'd trust me in my capacity as messenger by this point, Linden."

"I'm sorry, Ash." Linden looked at the ground and knotted their hands behind their back. "It's not that I don't trust you—"

"I know. It's just that you need a rationale for everything," said Ash. "Isn't that right? Earth is the most *crude* and *concrete* of the elements, after all. The *least* spiritually attuned. It only makes sense—it's your nature." They stroked Linden's cheek, turning their hand, and scraping Linden's skin with the sharp parts of their rings. Linden winced.

"Come," said Ash. "I can give you an explanation. We'll hold a sermon beneath the Auspicious Window in five minutes. River, fetch your Book."

"Yes, sir!" said River.

"No 'sir's, River. We're equals here," said Ash. But they smiled, and River knew that they had liked the "sir." River ran upstairs to fetch his Book from its place between the rusting lion-feet of the tub.

The room of the Auspicious Window had changed in the weeks since Linden's first visit, in no small part thanks to Linden's help supplying materials for its decoration. Two black-dyed bed sheets taped together lay spread across the floor, surrounded by a motley assortment of small rugs and cushions. Working as a team, Ash and River and Linden had moved a heavy round oak table from the upstairs bedroom to a place of pride beneath the Window, where it had become an altar. Candy fragments of filtered sunshine stained the objects laid reverently upon its dark, shiny surface: a spare teacup on a saucer, filled with water from the stream that ran on the other side of the woods. A crude human figure made of twigs bound together with string. Ash's collection of stones and shells and crystals. An assortment of Bic lighters. Several half-melted candles stuck in empty bottlenecks. More candles in amber. Green, blue, and clear glass bottles were arranged in the narrow floor space left between the sheets and the walls.

Regal and holy, Ash stood before the altar. Their hair was dappled in rainbows. Linden had arranged themself casually a few feet back from Ash, half-reclining, propped up on one arm and a leaking brocade pillow. River hurried to sit beside Linden, so that they could share his Book. Ash kept saying that they were going to make another Book for Linden, but they hadn't been able to get around to it yet.

Ash, of course, needed no Book to remind them of the truth and the way of things: Ash saw visions and spoke to angels. The Book was like training wheels for River's spiritual sense, Ash had explained, until he could do the same.

Until he really remembered who and what he was.

"River," said Ash. "Linden. Please turn to the first page of your Book."

River did so, and Linden looked on in what River now recognized as wry skepticism.

The first several pages of the Book were filled with Ash's writing on notebook paper, photocopied so that the lines of the paper showed dark and a little blurry. The words weren't in Ash's usual handwriting, but in a careful block print designed to render their meaning unmistakable. It reminded River of the writing exercises he'd done in kindergarten. "Read to us from the beginning, Linden," Ash said, schoolteacher-ish and seductive, their voice a caress.

"Okay." Linden took the Book from River's hands. "Let's see. Uh... 'The first things that existed in the universe were what we call, for lack of a better word, angels. The angels were not born and cannot die. They have no visible shape, no tangible form. They are many, but they lack individuality. They are not gods and they are not subjects of a God. They are the impulse and the act of creation and change. Their purpose is to alter matter and energy. From the first, they wanted to create thinking beings with faculties that mirrored those of the angels themselves. Eventually they did. Human beings stand proud and alone upon the surface of this angel-haunted world, in this cosmos of wild experiment.'"

Ash nodded. "Continue."

"'But human beings lost their way. They engaged in stagnant and destructive behavior. They had no regard for their fellow life forms. The angels didn't want to destroy them, but they could not force them to act differently. They could not even communicate with most humans, most of the time. As the universe moved farther and farther away from itself over billions of years, the angels had spread out too and become much weaker. They understood that what humans needed was a concentrated power that could direct them, that could speak to them and touch them and stay their hands. That would focus all its energies on changing and healing the damaged Earth. They needed a God. The angels would have to construct one for them.'"

"All right," said Ash. "That's good. That's enough. River? In your own words, will you tell us how the angels made a God?"

"Um," said River, unprepared. "Well. They took, like, parts of... themselves? ...And they put them together to create, like, new souls that could exist inside a body, that could have individual identity while remaining connected to the... thing. The angelic overmind. There were four souls, tuned to resonate with earth, with water, with air, and with fire. When the four souls all came together, they would be God. But the angels didn't realize how powerful flesh was. The flesh overwhelmed the special souls. They became corrupt and lost their memories. They thought that they were regular people."

Ash took over. "Yes. Until the vessel of fire—host to the strongest of God's elemental components, and the closest to the angels' original nature—had a vision one day, and remembered. And began to forge a path ahead, under angelic instruction. And began to gather the others. Someday, perhaps someday soon, the vessel of air will come to us, and we will all ascend. We will remake the world in a more perfect form. Until that day, I must instruct you two and try to help you remember what you are. The robes are part of the instruction. By becoming aware of your sweat and stink, the excretions and leakage of your human body, you will become better able to see your flesh component for what it is. A dumb, beastly mass that should be subservient to your spirit nature, not its jailer."

River nodded. Linden breathed out heavily through their nostrils, looking unimpressed, and River nodded more vociferously to make up for their insouciance. Ash crouched on the floor, so they could peer into Linden's eyes.

"Linden? Does it make sense to you now?" Their face bobbed so close to Linden's that, for a moment, River was certain Ash was about to either kiss or bite them.

"Sure, Ash," said Linden. "Sure, it makes sense."

They all sat in silence for a long stretch of moments. River watched dust float in shafts of stained glass light. The crystals and stones on the table looked alive, on the verge of movement. He could hear Ash and Linden breathing at each other, out of sync. He flipped through the Book until he found the colored-in Blake drawings again, and he stared hard at the one Ash had labeled as him, willing it to be true. Willing his dumb, beastly mass to assume that shape.

"River?" Ash finally spoke. "Will you light the candles on the altar? I'll make us drinks."

"Of course! Right away, sir!"

This time, Ash didn't correct him.

Later, after the lighting of candles and the sun tea mixed with vodka in the blue china cups, cleaner now than they'd once been—after the dimming of the day and the slow swirl of caffeine and alcohol engulfing their blood and brains, the loosening tensions, the lightness in their hearts and limbs. After rivulets of wax poured thick down every bottleneck in the room and it was hard to see the patterns of the Auspicious Window at all. After Ash had promised Linden over and over to copy a second Book for them, and Linden had promised with equal fervor to pay for the photocopying, or get it done for free, even—Linden knew a guy who worked at Kinko's. After Ash had danced for everyone, and River had made them all laugh when he let a cockroach crawl along his arm and said he'd like to keep it as a pet. Later, after a long and lovely afternoon, sometime in the early dark, Ash and Linden stood up from the black sheets, and embraced, and said they were going to bed. River knew what that meant. He nodded, and pretended to be engrossed in a search for more roaches.

Two sets of footsteps creaked up the stairs. One heavy and exuberant, one light and methodical. River thought about all the nights he'd spent curled in his tub, listening through the wall. Imagining the movements of his best friend and his… whatever Linden was. His rival? Ghostly halos of flame-light flickered on the walls. A muffled giggle trickled through a crack in the ceiling. A sigh. The sound of something soft collapsing to the floor. River tucked his Book beneath his arm and blew all the candles out. There was just enough moonlight leaking into the house for him to make his way up to the bathroom without difficulty. He put the Book back where it belonged and sat cross-legged on the cool tile, not sleepy at all.

The sounds were beginning in earnest. Ash and Linden could have been nocturnal animals locked in combat, a strangler and his victim shoving against each other. Members of the congregation at River's parents' church, seized suddenly by the Holy Spirit and compelled to writhe. To moan and speak in tongues. River was seized by something too: an impulse to see. It wasn't wrong, he told himself—according to Ash, they were all three of them part of one God, anyway. Perhaps knowing what Ash and Linden's congress actually looked like would torment him less than having to imagine it from auditory input alone. A hundred possible combinations of skin and spit and slick vaginal fluid playing on a loop in his brain until dawn.

He crept out the cracked bathroom door on all fours. The sounds grew louder. Still crouching, River carefully turned the cut-glass knob on the door to the bedroom. He used his other hand to push the door open, just a little bit. Just a crack to which he could put an eye. The sagging mattress of the big bed was in motion. A pair of flat feet with hairy ankles dangled over the edge. A pair of high-arched feet waved in the air above them, crossing and uncrossing.

River had to stand, slowly, heart hammering, so he could watch the action on the bed. Linden was stretched out on their back, mostly lost to shadow. Besides Linden's feet, River could see a slice of their muscled stomach illuminated by the moonlight coming in through the bedroom's tall, curtainless window. Linden had a very slight bulge of fat at the top of their hips. A small, stretched-out navel. It marked the beginning of a thick hair-trail, leading to a tangled black bush that spilled out onto Linden's upper thighs. On one of those thighs, a long, thin, white hand gripped hard enough to leave marks. Between the thighs, Ash's auburn curls bobbed and trembled, thrust forward insistently, nodded up and down. Linden's hands came up to clasp Ash's skull.

River could see Ash's long spine, their barely-there ass with a deep dimple above each butt cheek. He could even see between Ash's legs in little flashes as they crossed and uncrossed, flexed and relaxed. Ash had a huge, swollen clit, really almost like a tiny penis, and they stroked it with the fingers of their free hand, thrusting their pelvis into the mattress again and again. Ash was so wet, they dripped silvery strands of mucus onto the bed. The room smelled like animal musk and crushed moss.

River's genitals ached. He rubbed them, his hand pressed into the thin cloth of his robe, worrying he might somehow leave a stain. Trying not to make any noise. Ash sounded like a cat lapping water. Linden spasmed convulsively, said Ash's name a few times, and gave a low, anguished cry. Almost a howl. Their torso popped up from the bed like a resurrected corpse, and River saw their face screwed up and ugly in the moonlight, a chiaroscuro mask of an old man. It was enough for River. Almost too much. He dropped back to his hands and knees and retreated to the bathroom, where he shucked his jacket and robe and crouched naked in the corner farthest from the wall he shared with the bedroom. He could still hear everything.

River squeezed his eyes shut and put his hand back

between his legs. He could feel his erection straining painfully into the air, engorged as Ash's—no, much bigger. But that was wrong: his clit was a tiny shred of a thing. He had no cock and he was wet, all melting inside, sticking one finger and then two between the lips of his vulva, wriggling them around. He was a deep lake filled with greedy fish, putting his head between Ash's legs while Ash ate out Linden. He was sucking at the juices there. He was a boy jacking off. He was a girl who wanted to be a boy jacking off to the thought of Ash's hand, no, *Linden's* hand, no, it was Ash's hand after all on his dick, moving swift and sure.

For a few minutes, River felt as though he had all the power Ash had promised him—as though his short, pudgy fingers could dig into the clay of his flesh and reshape it, redirect its currents, transform it into anything he wanted. His own outline wavered and morphed in his mind's eye as he pushed, and spasmed, and, unlike the lovers beyond the wall, cried out not at all.

When he was done, he settled himself between the layers of blanket and sleeping bag in the tub. He lay awake and staring into the dark until he heard Linden take their leave.


The next day was excruciating. River couldn't stop thinking about what he'd seen. Every time he looked at Ash, his brain superimposed their naked body on top of the shapeless red robe in a kind of pseudo x-ray vision. Linden did not come to visit in the morning, nor in the afternoon, but reminders of their presence abounded: the sandwiches and bottled water Ash and River had for lunch. Ash drawing and making notes using the paper and colored pencils Linden had left behind. Linden's robe folded and neatly set on the smaller of the ex-bedroom tables, now located by the front door. River used half of his bottled water to rinse out the teacups, then decided to take a walk outside, hoping it would clear his mind. He didn't enjoy wearing shoes, but he planned to go into town, so he laced his boots over bare feet and stomped off through the wild field of grass and flowers, through the trees and up the long dirt path.

In town, River took advantage of the biggest service station's shower facilities (meant for long-haul truckers, he assumed) to wash himself and his underwear. Of course, then he had to put on his dirty, smelly robe and not-much-better army jacket again, so it only helped so much. Still, he looked better and hoped he'd be less conspicuous when he went to steal supplies from the Publix supermarket.

No such luck. Publix wasn't very busy, and River's slouchy, shifty manner and ragged appearance immediately attracted the attention of a stern-looking woman in an employee's vest. She tailed River through the aisles until, finally, he left with empty hands and pockets. He watched his shadow float beneath him as he crossed the parking lot. A bird sang nearby.

Across the road from Publix, small but neat houses sat in a cheerful pastel row, like crayons in a box. River wondered if Linden lived in any of them. He had no idea—Linden might live in a dorm, or in an apartment, or in a house with friends or family. Surely they'd talked about it at some point, but River often tuned Linden out, and he never asked them questions about their life.

Thoughts of Linden turned to thoughts of Linden and Ash fucking, and River grimaced at himself. His heart dipped low. Taking a walk had been useless, aside from the shower.

River slowly made his way back to the house in the woods. He tried to focus on the small, bright details of early spring: flowers opening their vivid petals to the high blue ceiling of the sky, a bird's nest with a length of neon cord threaded through its woven twigs. Little boys drawing with chalk in a driveway. An intensely yellow plastic bag soaring above the rooftops on a gust of wind. An osprey perched on a lamppost, fiercely surveying its domain. A group of punks with heavily patched clothes smoking in an alley, one of them tagging symbols on the brick side of a building. The elegant drapery of Spanish moss, and the green tunnel of trees that led to Ash and River's sanctuary. It didn't work.

River's eyes snagged on a used condom lying draped across a sewer grate. His ears pricked when one of the punks laughed loudly and, for a moment, sounded exactly like Linden. The fierce regard of the osprey reminded River of Ash, and he wondered if Ash knew he'd watched them fucking the previous night. River's cheeks burned. Ash hadn't spoken much to him yet today. Were they just distracted, or were they angry? What would they say on his return? What if Linden was there by the time he got back? What if they were both waiting to confront him? Worse, what if they didn't? What if they both knew he'd watched them and they just didn't care? What if River was too small, too young, too incidental to matter to Ash and Linden's love affair in any way?

*Maybe things will change when the vessel of air shows*

*up,* River thought. *Maybe Linden will get bored and go away and Ash will realize they weren't the vessel of earth after all.* His boots crunched over dry leaves, squelched through mud, shuffled through the occasional patch of gritty sand and sharp pebbles.

By the time River pushed the front door open and removed his boots, he was in a worse mood than ever. He needed Ash to rebuke him, to praise him, to give him a task. To do something that would reassure him of his worth.

"Ash?" he called into the house. "Hey, Ash?"

No answer. He walked through the room with the armchair, the room of the altar and the Auspicious Window. He went upstairs and checked the bedroom. He peered into the kitchen, where the plants in the sink looked bigger and more lush than ever before. Ash and Linden had been watering them, giving them new soil. All was quiet, deserted. River's heart sank.

"Ash? Ash?" he called, all but running through the back door and into the other side of the yard. "Ash! Please, Ash? Where are you?"

Ash was standing at the edge of the yard, knee-deep in grass and flowers, motionless, staring into space with their head cocked like they were listening to something. Their eyes were flat mirrors, the same color as the sky.

"Ash!" River felt sticks and stones scratch at the soles of his feet, maybe even breaking the skin, drawing blood. He didn't care. He rushed to Ash's side and touched his friend's arm. Ash's flesh was warm and pliant, but they didn't move or respond.

River put his arms around Ash's waist and held them. He closed his eyes and breathed in Ash's scent. Ash smelled more sour than most people, River thought, but in a good way. A sweetish way, like lightly rotting lemons. He stayed pressed to Ash's back until he felt their body shift beneath him. Then he gently pulled away and said their name again.

"River!" Ash turned to him, surprised and happy. "Where have you been?"

"Where have *you* been? I came back from a gas station shower and you were in one of your trances. You didn't say anything when I called for you, and I had to look all through the house... I thought maybe you'd *left*. For good, I mean."

"Oh, River." Ash chuckled. "Why would I ever do that?"

"I don't know! I'm not you! Maybe... I imagined for a minute that you might've gone to Linden's. That they'd told you where they live and had invited you to stay."

Ash shook their head in wry amusement. They tousled River's clean hair. "*No*, silly boy. You've got it backwards. This is our temple and our home. I don't belong in a house full of worldly students with Linden—Linden belongs *here*, with us. In fact." Ash took a breath. "The angels have been speaking to me all day. They tell me, and I agree, that it's time to take the next step. Linden is beginning to wake up. They accept my authority, they're not skeptical. Linden understands what and who they are and what we are. River." Ash smiled, dimpled, glowed. "The next time Linden visits, I'm going to ask them to move in with us."

River's mouth hung open. He blinked rapidly. Then, unable to quite credit his ears and overtaken by a surge of helpless, despairing hilarity, he began to laugh.

He snorted, doubled over, and he was horrified but he couldn't stop himself. The laughter spilled from between his teeth like vomit.

"River," asked Ash, not cold or angry but sounding truly confused, "River, why in the world is that funny? You know it's foreordained. We need to gather together in one place to await the vessel of air and our joint ascension. The final days."

"I know, I know," River choked out. "But Linden doesn't! Oh my god, you think, you think, you..." He was overcome by another wave of hysteria. Deep in the recesses of his physical self, a tiny part of River's consciousness begged him to stop, to straighten up and have faith in Ash. To infer exactly what Ash needed to hear and then say that, only that, with just the right combination of solemnity and adoration on his face.

"What do I think, River? Tell me."

The tiny scrap of River begging for self-control lost its fight. Words flew from inside him, almost gleeful, interspersed with more hiccuping laughter.

"Linden came in to talk to me yesterday, you know? They came in to talk to me alone. Linden's not going to live with us, Ash! They think this place is filthy! They think it's disgusting! They feel sorry that we have to live here, like this—that's why they're always bringing us things! Linden told me they don't believe in *anything* you say, not in vessels for elemental spirits, or in being parts of God, or in angels, or in power, or in the final days! They only go along with all this stuff because it makes you happy, and they think you're a *great fuck!*" He finished out of breath, howling, sides aching as though he'd run a mile.

"That's wrong," they said softly. Ash's face was as inscrutable as an unpainted plaster statue's. "That's not true, River. You're saying false things to hurt me. Something dark has gotten into you, some flesh-demon, and it's making you turn against us."

"I'm not turned against you!" River struggled to regain his composure and succeeded a little. "I'm really not! I've always loved you. I've always believed you. I've always been totally loyal to you! It's *Linden* who doesn't take you seriously, and—"

Ash slapped River hard across the face. He reeled backward from the shock and fell on his ass, crushing wildflowers beneath him. Both stared at the other with wide, hurt eyes.

River had been slapped in the face plenty often in his (almost) sixteen years, but not by Ash. Ash had never been violent to him, nor even threatened violence, and River had let his guard down with Ash. Had come to believe that, even if he upset his friend, physical attacks were off the table in their relationship.

What an idiot he'd been. One of Ash's rings had cut River's face, just below his left eye. He felt a tiny stream of hot blood start to roll down his cheek. It mixed with tears as it went. Ash stood above him, still looking surprised, not offering to help him, nor apologizing. River scrambled up and tore off across the field, heedless of his aching sides and bare feet. He passed the house, entered the trees on its opposite side, whipped in the face and thighs by branches. Not looking back, not caring where he was going. Not even when he heard Ash's voice calling his name over and over in the distance.

IV. The angels were braided through everything, holding it up and tearing it apart, whispering through the cells of the world wherever Ash went, but sometimes they commanded attention, and other times they faded into the background. As the sunset dyed the sky from blue to pink, the angels faded, their faces and wheels and dripping intestines becoming jessamine blossoms and cotton-candy clouds. Anthills and pine branches. The small voice gnawing at the back of Ash's mind belonged to Ash. It insisted that they go and search for River, who had not returned after he'd stormed off in a childish fit of pique hours earlier. *After you hit him,* Ash's inner voice corrected.

*No,* Ash argued back. *After he provoked me into hitting him.* They raked a hand through their hair, making sure to dig their nails into their scalp so hard, it hurt.

Ash didn't hit people. Ash wasn't violent; they had never believed in violence, nor needed it to get their way. But Ash had hit River. Gentle River, so small and young, whom they loved and had vowed to protect. But it was River's fault, wasn't it? He'd said such awful things about Linden. They were all lies, of course. Linden loved Ash. Linden revered Ash. Ash was sure it was so—if it hadn't been, they'd have felt it. All those times with their fingers inside Linden, or their tongue...

Still watching the sky anxiously, Ash leaned their elbows on the porch railing. It made a mushy, ominous noise and the texture was unpleasant against Ash's bare skin. They didn't move: the texture was penance for letting River tempt them into losing their temper. Linden hadn't yet come to visit that day, and Ash was beginning to think that Linden probably wouldn't come.

That was all right; Linden didn't visit every day. They still had obligations to the outside world. Hadn't yet been brave enough to relinquish their old life. Although Ash thought Linden was ready to take that step—if not now, then very soon. Perhaps they were only waiting for Ash's permission, Ash's encouragement. Yes, sang the angels in their shuddering, muffled chorus. *Yes, yes, yes.*

*Linden's not going to come,* said the reproachful voice inside Ash's skull. *Go and look for River. What if he's lost? What if he's contrite, but too frightened to return in case you don't forgive him? You have a responsibility to the boy.*

"I do," Ash agreed out loud. "I *do* have a responsibility."

River was like the younger brother Ash had never had, or the son, or the something even more precious and intimate. Sometimes, looking at their sweet little boy huddled in that too-big army jacket like a kitten in a blanket, Ash was overwhelmed by a sense that they had personally created him—molded his round cheeks and delicate chin from wet clay with their hands and breathed life into his inert organs with their lips. Imagined each detail of his personality and his past to complement Ash's desires for a companion and a family. Ash didn't think they had really made River like a golem. It was just a feeling. But it was a feeling with a lot of truth in it. Where would the poor kid be now if Ash had never met him? Never shown him the way, named him and given him a purpose?

*He'd be nowhere and nothing,* sang the angels. *Raped and murdered. Left by the roadside. Down deep beneath the ground.*

The sky was almost entirely the color of milkweed

flowers, gilded at the edges. Ash pushed themself back to a fully standing position. They stepped off the porch. It was time to start looking for River. All afternoon, Ash had thought that he'd eventually wander back on his own, but by now, they were consumed by a conviction that if they did not seek him out and bring him home themself, the boy would never return. To lose River—that any part of God should separate from the others once it had found its way to them—was blasphemy. Ash winced. It was painful to entertain such thoughts.

No need to entertain them, then. Ash would succeed in their mission tonight, as they succeeded in all things.

Ash stalked off into the tall grass, quick and quiet as any apex predator. The angels chimed encouragement from all sides as they moved away from the sacred place and entered the shade of the trees. The growing dusk.

By the time it had been full dark for an hour, Ash was frustrated, bored, and confused. They had scoured the woods all the way to the stream and the little swampland that abutted the highway. The impassive glowing eyes of angels and alligators alike scrutinized Ash from the muck as they called River's name. Assuring him that they were no longer angry. Reminding him of where he belonged, and that he'd left most of his possessions back at the house, including his boots.

Once the sky was lavender and Ash had made a circuit back to the clearing, they were forced to accept two possibilities: either River had hidden himself so well that even Ash, with all their insight and angelic assistance, couldn't find him, or he had abandoned the safety of the trees and gone into town.

Ash had neatened themself as best they could, tying their hair back with a scrap of fabric and splashing their face with the last of the bottled water. They belted their robe at the waist and put their patchwork vest on over it, to make the robe look more like an ordinary garment. Then, still confident, they headed for the walking path, taking the same route River had taken much earlier in the day.

Now the sky was indigo verging on a starry black. Ash had been wandering the neon-drizzled streets of the town for quite some time, and they were starting to get a headache. They'd seen no sign of River, and were beginning to realize just how monumental a task it would be to search for him here. True, a college town was not a city—and Ash had lived in plenty of cities—, but it was big enough for a boy to get lost in.

The streets were laid out in a haphazard spiderweb of dead ends and sudden turns, very unlike the sensible urban grids to which Ash was more accustomed. Angels drooled and twitched and giggled in the mind-altering electric buzz of liquor store and 24-hour convenience signs. Young people stood in exuberant knots mid-sidewalk, taking up too much space. Chatting and smoking. A tiny lizard darted across the pavement, begging to be stepped on in the dimness. Some kids in their early teens were doing skateboard tricks in the shelter of a mostly-empty concrete parking garage. River was absent from every scene, and Ash was reduced to silent visual scanning, unable to call his name lest they attract unwanted attention. Closing their eyes for a moment, Ash rubbed their temples with their forefingers. It was all too much. They begged the angels, the universe, their own fiery nature, for a sign, a clue, *something*.

"...No, Nora, don't be ridiculous. I mean, c'mon."

Linden's voice.

Ash's eyes flicked open. What was Linden doing here? they thought for a split second. Then: of course Linden was here. Linden lived in town. Linden did not cease to exist whenever they left Ash for a night or for a few nights.

Ash saw Linden coming towards them down the sidewalk. They looked different in a baggy T-shirt and corduroy pants, a snapback cap on their head. Linden was engrossed in conversation with a large, dark young woman who frowned skeptically at them. Ash thought she looked like a goth bank teller. Neither Linden nor their friend had seen them, and Ash immediately decided that it would be best for them to continue unobserved. They sidled into a convenient alleyway and stood, back pressed against the bricks, waiting for the pair to pass. Angels swiveled incorporeal finger-manifestations in Ash's pores from their perches on the breeze. On the mortar of the alley wall.

"Linden," the goth bank teller was saying. "Don't bullshit me. Something's been up the past few weeks. Okay, maybe it's not drugs. But you're cagey, you don't want to go out most nights, and you're still always tired in the morning. You've been skipping classes, which isn't like you—"

"You're not my mother, Nora."

"Fuck no, I'm not your mother! But I'm your friend! I care about you! I want to know what's happening in your life, and if you have any problems you need help with... Linden, you used to tell me *everything*."

"There's always been stuff I've kept to myself. Maybe you just didn't notice it before."

Ash strained to make out Nora's response, but it was inaudible. They were just ahead of their hiding place now and Ash thought fast. Linden and the goth bank teller—Nora—were evidently preoccupied. There were plenty of deep shadows. Little alleys and conveniently placed shrubs on the streets ahead. Ash had power, and the prodding angel-fingers urged them on. They could follow the two unnoticed, see where they went. Perhaps River too, would be drawn towards Linden. Perhaps River had even sought Linden out already, and would be waiting for them at their place of residence. Ash recalled that Linden lived in some sort of housing co-op in the downtown area. It wouldn't be far. Ash slipped from the alleyway, willing themself to melt invisibly into the warm night.

The house where Linden lived was shabby, though not nearly as shabby as Ash and River's house in the woods. The tiny strip of front lawn it had was scraggly with dead yellow grass and scattered with dog turds, but the front porch was large and inviting, filled with mismatched, comfortable-looking chairs. A wooden sign hung above the front door, with big, elaborately serifed letters burned into it: BUG HOUSE.

Bug House was tall and narrow. A similar, albeit more reputable-looking, house flanked it on one side. A lumpy driveway filled with cars and bicycles, leading to a small detached garage, sat on the other. There was a fence on the garage side of the yard too—a gap-toothed grin of faded white pickets. Beyond the fence was only a vacant lot.

Lights and noise and chatter emanated from Bug House's ground floor. Flashing red glimmer, sounds of barking dogs and caterwauling guitars. Some sort of party was going on. A few figures stumbled out onto the front porch and lit cigarettes—no, those were joints. The tangy reek of marijuana hit Ash's nose in a rush as they hunkered down at the edge of the vacant lot, just behind the fence.

River was nowhere to be seen, and now that Ash had arrived at Bug House, they didn't think River would be inside. He was a shy, sensitive child, averse to strangers, crowds, cacophony, and any intoxication beyond a two-drink buzz. During their nomad months, Ash had often had to cajole him to participate in even small, laid-back gatherings of new acquaintances.

Nora and Linden waved to the people on the porch, then turned to walk down the driveway. Ash's heart pounded. River might still be lost, but Ash had been called here for a reason. Surely they needed to hear whatever it was that Linden had to say to their friend.

Ash pressed close to the fence and followed Nora and Linden to the mouth of the garage. Peered through a convenient hole in the peeling wood. The two shadowy figures quietly resumed their argument.

"Linden," Nora said. "Please. Either tell me what's been going on with you, what's got you so distracted recently, always disappearing off to God-knows-where, or tell me *why* you won't tell me. If you give me a reason for keeping it to yourself, I'll respect your right to privacy. But you can't gaslight me by saying nothing's changed—"

"For fuck's sake, I'm not *gaslighting* you. I'm not trying to make you think you're crazy! You're not crazy! I just don't see why I should have to tell you anything!"

Good, thought Ash, who had gathered what this conversation must be about. Nora is an outsider. *Dull flesh, insensible to angels. She'd never understand, and she doesn't need to hear. Not yet. Hold fast, Linden.*

"I thought we had an intimate relationship," Nora was saying.

"*You* thought—Nora, *you're* the one who's always insisted that we're just friends! Just friends who fuck sometimes!"

Ash frowned. Pressed closer to the gap. Splintery angel-shards mashed into the skin around their eye. Nora and Linden were standing very close to each other, arguing like two birds or cats trying to intimidate one another by puffing up. Linden had a couple inches of height on Nora, but Nora definitely possessed the advantage in bulk. Linden kept gesturing with their arms far out to the side as if to make up for it, while Nora rocked forward on her toes when she spoke.

"I don't want to be in a monogamous partnership right now!" she hissed. "I don't want to do romance! But there's no 'just' about our friendship, Linden. Don't insult me. I care about my friends more than anything in the world, and you've been my friend since freshman year. I've always trusted you with my problems, and you've always trusted me with yours. We help each other. Isn't that right?"

"You're drowning in friends," said Linden. "Friends and friends' problems. Why would I want to burden you more? I'm not even having a problem right now. I got into something stupid. Just as a lark. It's not serious, it's nothing—I'll be over it soon. The glamor's already wearing off."

Ash ground their fingernails into the palms of their hands until it hurt. They gritted their teeth. Linden was lying to get this obsessed woman to stop asking invasive questions. That had to be it.

"You know," Nora sighed. "That's the exact wrong thing to say if you want to convince me you're not dabbling in heroin." Ash wasn't sure, but they thought they saw her smile.

"I promise I've never done heroin," Linden murmured. They reached out to touch Nora's shoulder and pull her even closer. "And I promise I still love you. I love you a lot more than any passing kick of mine."

Nora cuddled into Linden and pulled their face down to hers. Linden embraced her passionately and the two kissed, open mouthed. They kept at it for a while, making small noises, their hands roaming over each others' backs.

Behind the fence, Ash trembled and clenched their hands tighter. They bit their lower lip until they tasted hot, coppery blood. The angels were screaming warning, betrayal. Ash felt that their eyes were about to explode into froth and jelly in their sockets. That their heart was about to collapse on itself. They pushed themself away from the fence, barely remembering to move quietly, and scuttled across the vacant lot on all fours. They had seen enough. More than enough. When they were about half a block from Bug House and safely out of Linden and Nora's sight, Ash stood and ran for the woods. Through the trees, through the mud, through the Spanish moss. Spiderwebs clung to Ash's face and arms, and they didn't bother brushing them away. Owls, or angels disguised with owl-voices, hooted from above. The night was blurred and wicked with the salt of blood and tears. Ash found themself grunting and growling. Pissed-off, wordless, animal sounds. They wanted to howl in the dark like a coyote. When they burst into the clearing, Ash saw candle flames flickering in the house's windows. River. He'd come home after all.

Ash wanted to pick up speed and tear across the wildflowers and long grass, to burst through the door with a bang. They forced themself to slow down instead—to stop making noise, stand tall and regain a little of their composure. They didn't want to scare the poor boy further, or give him any more cause for doubt. Ash needed to think. As they made their way to the house, they listened closely to the angels, and to the small voice at the back of their skull. By the time they had the rusted doorknob in their hand, they knew what they had to do. How they could fix everything. It would be difficult, but they had guidance. Encouraging whispers came from all directions to support them in their purpose. Thank you, Ash thought out into the wide world. Aloud, they called, "River? I'm home," as they stepped inside. There, they saw the edge of River's aura, lovely deep green, but stained with rotten patches, tremble at their approach. He was in the room of the Auspicious Window.

"River? I know you're there. Don't be afraid, sweet boy. I have such important news!"

# PART TWO

The flowering of flesh is like the
flowering of grass

**I.** It had been three days since Ash had told River about the new ceremony. River wasn't sure if he was more worried that it would never really happen—or more worried that it would. "You were right," Ash had proclaimed, bursting into the room of the Auspicious Window on Sunday night. River failed to flinch only because he had, uncharacteristically, helped himself to several long gulps of vodka prior to Ash's return. His friend looked deranged by candlelight, wisps of curl zig-zagging out of a low, loose ponytail to frame their too-bright eyes like threads of smoke. Shadows made a skull of their sharp features. "Right about what?" River asked, averting his eyes. "Not *right*, exactly," Ash continued, seeming not to hear him. "I mean, you were more correct than I was. I was *wrong* earlier, is the thing. When we fought. I was wrong, and I'm sorry. I shouldn't have accused you of any malign influence. You were only trying to warn me."

"I..." River started. "Wait. Is this about Linden?" He gingerly brushed the side of his face where Ash's ring had gashed him beneath his eye. It had begun to swell.

"Yes!" Ash strode to River's side and gracefully folded their body beside him on the nest of pillows he'd made. They took his hands in theirs. He felt the metal of their rings and the bones of their knuckles before he felt the warm smoothness of their skin. He wanted to recoil, but didn't dare. River made himself look steadily into Ash's eyes. Their pupils were blown and glossy. He made himself think about how beautiful Ash was.

"Yes," said Ash again. "I have received messages tonight. Linden believes. I am sure that Linden believes, deep down. But their faith may be faltering. They're conflicted, pulled between their true nature and the worldly obligations they think they still must shoulder." Ash smiled at River. "Obligations such as you and I have never felt, kiddo. That's one respect in which our disenfranchisement has blessed us."

River didn't feel very blessed at the moment, but his mood lifted a bit to hear Ash doubting Linden—placing themselves with River on one side of a divide, and Linden on the other. If Ash continued in this vein, River thought, he'd forgive them anything and everything.

"I'm sorry I told you that Linden only... only liked you for sex," he said. "I was upset. I didn't mean it, really. Linden doesn't understand you, but they're not a total dick."

"I know," said Ash, squeezing River's small palms. "I know. That's why we can't invite Linden to live with us—"River's heart leapt, a joyous fish in the salt sea of his body, "—before we've given them a test," Ash finished. "In fact, we must all undergo a test, and soon. A trial."

River frowned. He imagined answering trivia questions about the Book, having to defend his belief and worthiness in front of a bewigged Ash holding a gavel. He recognized these thoughts as stupid, childish wordplay, but he couldn't picture anything else.

"What kind of test do you mean?"

Ash grinned, and for a moment, their face was a death's head again.

"In ancient times, all sorts of cultures used plants and fungi to compromise their fleshly defenses and allow them communion with higher planes of existence. Such rituals allowed witches and shamans to prove their faith; their mettle and their readiness to assume a sacred post. We, who are so much more than mere witches and shamans, should surely hold ourselves to at least as rigorous a standard."

"Wait. You want us to do *drugs*? Ash, I don't know. I mean, booze is one thing, but I've never... I don't even like pot! It makes me all shaky and paranoid, and sometimes I think I hear voices—"

"The voices of the angels," Ash soothed. "Which you'll hear all the time soon enough, as I do. You're *supposed* to hear them, River. Anyway, we should make haste with this ritual. I know what we need. I've already got most of it, and I can procure the rest quickly. All will be ready by Tuesday evening, and the next time Linden visits after that—whether it be morning, midday, or night—the three of us will drink together. A new drink, for a new, more serious covenant." Ash squeezed River's hands again. They leaned closer to his face. "Do you trust me?"

River swallowed.

He squeezed back.

"Of course."

River did trust Ash. He *did*. But a gray heaviness grew in his stomach through Monday and Tuesday and Wednesday. Ash didn't bother preaching to River or talking him through ceremonies of burning small objects and burying them and immersing them in water. Ash didn't light the candles in the room of the Auspicious Window or stand before the altar. They didn't go out to wash themselves, to procure food or cash, to visit the public library and use the computers or read books from the Occult section.

Ash did go out though, more often and for longer periods of time than usual, bringing home things that unsettled River: ugly, skinny dried mushrooms in a Baggie, what seemed to be hundreds and hundreds of little black seeds wrapped in a red handkerchief. Ash picked an armload of jessamine flowers from the yard and left them in a wilting pile beside the dank, wild garden of the kitchen sink. Ash collected leaves from the woods, all kinds of leaves.

On Monday night they used their mortar and pestle to crush some of them. River watched, curled into the armchair he'd adopted as his favorite spot. As Ash ground the fat, phallic stone against the long, smooth leaves in the bowl, a sharp, sweet smell cut through the comforting leaf mould and rain scent of the chair's upholstery.

River sniffed the air.

"It's like... cocktail cherries," he observed. "Weird. Nice."

"Some say it's more like almonds," said Ash. "But yes. They call it the Carolina Laurelcherry for a reason."

"Is that for us? For the ritual?"

"It's for the ritual, but not for us." Ash beat the Carolina Laurelcherry paste with aggressive enthusiasm until its strange perfume seemed a sticky, invisible layer coating every surface in the living room. "You and I and Linden—three parts with three different elemental natures. We'll all need different formulas."

"That makes sense."

River bit his lip.

He hoped Ash couldn't see the gray heaviness in his aura. That it wasn't an obvious stain eating away the pure parts of him like an emotional cancer. "Will Linden come tomorrow, do you think? They weren't here Sunday, and they weren't here today, and they've never skipped more than two days in a row before."

"Linden will come." Ash nodded. "Linden will come, assuredly. But River..."

"Yes?"

"If by some chance they don't come by tomorrow afternoon, I need you to get me some distilled water. *Distilled* water. Not tap, not sparkling. In a bottle. This is very important."

"Okay." River thought for a moment. "If I do that, can I... can I wear my regular clothes? The robe attracts too much attention in stores." *And it stinks. And it looks like a dress. And I hate wearing it,* he added silently. Then he mentally rebuked himself. He imagined Ash slapping him in the face again.

"Yes," Ash said. "Of course you should change your clothes to go out and get the water. You don't need my permission to change your clothes." They stopped grinding and put the bowl of paste aside. Stood up, brushing off their robe's now-ragged skirt. "I mean, obviously it would be best, if you must change, to revert to your holy garment as soon as you re-enter the house. These things do matter to the world—to the angels. To your own energy." They rolled their eyes piously up at the moisture-blotched ceiling.

"Sure." River curled deeper into the chair, suddenly sick of the cherry smell, trying to escape it to no avail.

"Also, if you do end up getting the water, could you pick up some food while you're at it? Cheese, crackers. Maybe some strawberries or citrus from that one yard near the elementary school and the Masonic temple, you know which I mean. Whatever's ripe."

"Sure, Ash. Sure."

Linden didn't come on Tuesday, and River did go on an all-afternoon mission to steal distilled water, snacks, and yard fruit. He reveled in the feel of his threadbare but clean-ish sweatpants against his leg hair, although it was almost too warm for them, especially with his jacket. When he came home, all his pockets were weighted down with bounty. He'd shoved two small bottles of distilled water into the waistband of his pants, where they were concealed by his too-big T-shirt, his jacket, and the fact that he was round and sort of lumpy in the middle.

"River, you're amazing," said Ash, after he'd set everything in neat rows on the countertop and floor for them. "You're fast and silent and flowing. No one can touch you and you take what you will. I'm proud." They hugged him close and breathed more kind words into his hair. They rubbed his back.

River allowed himself to imagine that Linden would never come back again, that Ash had seen that he was growing up, finally—that Ash would see they were wrong about needing any other people. That Ash and River were one complete unit, one full soul all by themselves. They could be happy, River thought. Happy like that. Forever. Seeing each other only through each others' eyes, deep in the woods. They could stop wearing robes and preparing for the final days.

Ash released River from the hug and held him out from their body at arm's length.

Their blue eyes sparkled.

"Soon," they said. "Soon, everything comes to fruition. The angels have told me. It's a howl on the air and a taste on my tongue. Linden isn't far. And once Linden's way has been corrected, once the three of us are together for good, the way shall be paved for the fourth chosen vessel. Oh, River. It's all so *close* now."

The fantasies vanished. The weight in River's stomach gathered itself, became darker and heavier. He knew Ash would be in a terrible state if Linden abandoned them now. He suspected that if Linden *did* turn up though, something bad would happen. He remembered the videos he'd had to watch in school, before he'd left: hokey twenty-year-old D.A.R.E. specials where kids with gel-spiked hair tried LSD and went insane. Jumped out of fifth-floor windows thinking they could fly. Had seizures and foamed at the mouth and suffered permanent brain damage when their drugs had been cut with something else, or when they misjudged a dose. When they didn't realize they were eating poison.

The videos were hokey, but they'd scared River anyway. He still had nightmares about some of them, the way he still had nightmares about Hell sometimes. Trust Ash, River commanded his mind, his heart, the thundercloud mass in his stomach. Ash is wise. *Ash wouldn't make a mistake like that.* It didn't work. River just felt even more sick, even more worried. Ash turned from him, back to work with hard black seeds and drooping yellow petals. Humming softly under their breath, ignoring him. The hours crept on, and on.

Finally, late on Wednesday, Linden showed up on the front porch of the house. They knocked shave-and-a-haircut on the door and sang a verse of "Bedlam Boys." Ash was off in the trees at the edge of the back yard, so River, who had been reading a crumbling paperback in his bathtub bed, came downstairs to greet Linden.

"You could've just come in," he said.

Linden hesitated before crossing the threshold. "It... wouldn't have felt right. Not this time. Where's Ash?"

"In back." River hitched a thumb. He was astounded at how calm he sounded. His insides felt like a disrupted wasp's nest. "I can go get them, if you want."

"Yeah," said Linden. They stood between the door and the foot of the stairs, fidgeting. They made no move to put on their brown robe, or to take off any of their street clothes, and avoided looking at River's face. "Yeah, thanks. That'd be good."

Would the ceremony happen now? Would it be deferred to another day at the last minute?

River was wasps buzzing and leaden gray weight sinking down, down, down as he trudged through the house and the yard to fetch Ash. He was a collage of fear and bad things coming, hardly a boy at all.

He had to pinch his skin to make sure it was still there.


The three elemental vessels sat in a circle on the floor. Kaleidoscope light danced into the room to cover them. The Auspicious Window was long and gilded behind Ash, who solemnly passed red Solo cups to River on their right and Linden on their left. Linden, who had steadfastly refused to change into their robe, shifted uncomfortably on the black sheet.

"Ash," they started, "it's very kind of you to invite me to tea again, but I really need to talk to you one on one about—" Linden cut their eyes at River. "About our, uh, visits. Our relationship."

"Yes." Ash smiled and nodded. "Of course. We'll have that conversation after we drink. No—" they put out a hand to stop Linden from taking a sip of their beverage, "I want us all to start together, at the same time. Wait."

Linden lowered their plastic cup. Dark yellowy-brown liquid sloshed against the sides. "What is this, again?" they asked. "It smells like maraschino cherries."

"That's what I said!" River lifted his own cup and took a sniff of his drink. He recoiled. "Ugh, but mine doesn't smell like that. Mine smells like dirt. Gross dirt."

"We're three different aspects of God, in three different vessels, with three different needs," Ash explained, again. "So I've prepared us three slightly different drinks. Don't worry. It's just a cold herbal tea."

"But you told me it was going to be—"

Ash brushed their forefinger against River's lips. "I changed my plan," they announced, looking at Linden, whose face was etched with doubt.

"Why are we drinking out of *these* things? Wouldn't the teacups be more special?" asked Linden, swirling their drink around, gazing into the whirlpool of it, and avoiding Ash's eyes.

"They're all broken," said Ash, calm and cool.

They weren't lying, either. River had watched them

hurl the teacups against the back wall of the house that morning, stomping on them in boots after each shattered. Making sure that the shards of blue china would never be anything whole again.

River looked into his own cup of liquid, breathing through his mouth so he didn't have to smell it. It was a darker brown than Linden's, muddy and full of black flecks floating around like dead flies.

"Now." Ash raised their cup high above their head, "We salute the angels."

River and Linden copied Ash's gesture. Their cups flanked Ash's in the air, spotlit by shafts of green and gold light.

"And we drink," said Ash. They brought their cup to their mouth and downed a long swallow. River and Linden followed suit.

River almost spat his out immediately. It tasted *foul*. Ash shot him a wicked glare.

"Keep drinking. You have to drink *all* of it, little River."

Linden had downed about half their cup and put it to the side. "Ash. Look, we've had our drinks, we did our ceremony, now let's go talk in private—"

"No," Ash interrupted. "You have to drink *all* of it, Linden. Then we can talk."

"Oh, for fuck's sake!" Linden burst out. They began to stand up. "I told you, I don't want any more! I'm done playing along with your weird little games, no matter how much fun we have in bed. Sorry, River," they added, with a guilty look in his direction.

"I know what sex is," mumbled River. Linden opened their mouth to say more, but Ash leapt forward and pushed them back down onto the sheet. Linden yelled and kicked, but Ash pinned their arms and straddled them. They sat back on Linden's thighs as River watched in shock and amazement. He drank more, and almost didn't taste it at all. Linden was strong and fit, visibly heavier and more muscular than Ash, but they seemed powerless to fend off their skinny attacker. Ash looked waifish holding Linden to the floor, as though Ash was the vulnerable one, the one under threat. Their pale eyes shimmered with rage and pain.

"Come help me, River. Get Linden's cup. Make them drink."

River idly thought about refusing, about leaving the room and letting Ash and Linden sort their own problems out. But Ash's voice was pleading. Their eyes were so hurt. Ash needed him.

River brought Linden's cup. He ignored Linden's begging and cursing. It felt like his hands weren't even his: they looked so small, so soft and plump, but they were so strong in action as they grabbed Linden's stubbly scalp, forced Linden's head back, and poured perfumed liquid into their mouth.

When Linden sputtered and gagged and squeezed their lips shut, he did what he'd seen in movies and held Linden's nose closed until their teeth gaped wide and their tongue lolled out to take the air, the drink. He massaged Linden's throat to make them swallow. Linden was crying. Their nose started to run, and they swallowed snot too. Salt water trickled between River's fingers, but he sensed it only in an abstract way. When he looked down, he was surprised to find that it was real. The tears were clear and pure. Linden's drink was all gone. Ash was practically lying down on top of Linden, still holding them fast.

River dropped the empty cup and let it roll into a corner, where it scared a fat spider out of its hiding place. He put his fingers to his mouth to taste Linden's tears. *Like the sea*, he thought, and he had a sudden yearning to go to the beach, to wander along a boardwalk and eat cotton candy.

"River," Ash admonished him. "Go and finish your drink now."

River obeyed. He plopped down a good distance from Linden, who wriggled and spat, and Ash, whose hair hung over their face in loose, tangled curls. Ash said nothing, and seemed to have a grasp as unyielding as steel or stone.

River watched them as though they were a far away and not especially interesting TV news broadcast. He took small sips of his drink and did his best not to retch at the godawful flavor, like what he imagined drinking liquid dogshit would taste like.

Time stretched out and seemed to still, to pool inside River's belly with the noxious black-flecked fluid. When there was nothing left in his cup, he let it roll away too, and he stared at his hands. They really were like the hands of a young child, he thought. Even the fingernails were tiny, blunt nubs. How had he held Linden's head that way, only moments ago? Could it really have been him? Was it possible he was dreaming, curled in the bathtub and the blankets with his paperback book laid open on his chest, its spine broken? River was beginning to feel very, very strange.

"Ash?" His voice emerged as a hoarse whisper, and

Ash gave no indication that they'd heard. "Ash?" he tried again, louder. Too loud. Both Ash and Linden started.

"What, River?" said Ash, annoyed, as they wrestled Linden back to the ground.

"You gave us hallucinogens after all, didn't you? I feel…"

"Jesus fucking Christ." Linden laughed hoarsely. "You dosed me with, what? Acid? Peyote? Some kind of vision quest plant? *Oh my god.*" Their arms and legs twisted, but they seemed to be losing energy, some of their ability to struggle.

"No," said Ash. "No." They turned briefly to River. "It shouldn't hit you for another several minutes. Whatever you feel now is something else." They blew a strand of hair out of their eyes. "Maybe you're finally starting to hear the angels."

River listened, but he heard nothing he would describe as angelic. The cut beneath his eye throbbed like a heart. He watched Linden beat the black-sheeted floor with their palms. River's hands were shaking a little, he noticed, and so were Linden's. Linden's hands were shaking more and more. Their feet, too.

"Fuck," Linden said. "Fuck fuck fuck fuck."

"Linden?" Ash released Linden and stood up. Stepped away. Linden's limbs jerked erratically as they stumbled, trying to rise. They seemed to unfurl in stop-motion as they got to their feet, where they swayed drunkenly.

"What'd you give me?!" Linden snarled. Then they coughed. They coughed again, doubling over, and almost fell. "Okay. Okay, I'm leaving." Staggering forward, they missed the doorway into the kitchen, hit the wall, and sank to their knees. "Fuck," they said again. "Ash? I don't think I can walk. I don't think... Ash, my vision's all blurry. My legs aren't working right."

"You'll have to stay here, then," Ash observed. "With us."

Linden's tears began anew.

"That's the last thing I need," they moaned. "Tripping in here..."

They laughed another humorless laugh, then coughed, gasped, coughed, coughed, hacked and wheezed. A long strand of pinkish drool spilled from their mouth, and they convulsed more and more. Laughing silently now. Laughing and crying at the same time. The drool had reached the floor, but the strand still led up, unbroken, to the inside of Linden's body.

River started to laugh too. It was pretty funny. Ash returned to their abandoned Solo cup and drank it dry in two swallows. They spun around in a circle, humming to themself, and then danced over to River. They tousled his hair.

"Easy, now," they murmured. "Don't choke yourself."

River tried to ease his laughter, but the effort only made him laugh even harder.

"S-sorry," he giggled, as Ash sat down beside him.

Linden was lying on their side now, heaving and undulating, fingers scrabbling against their face and chest, wide-eyed, leaking pink from their nose and mouth. Their tongue poked out from between their teeth and lips. It was suddenly bright, bright red, like they'd been sucking on a Jolly Rancher.

"*Cherry,*" River gasped. "It's cherry flavored!"

He dissolved into laughter again.

Now tears were leaking through his eyelashes, too. River howled.

"Shh," said Ash, pulling him close, cuddling him as he shook. "Yes. Cherry. It was hard, but we did it. Now everything will be fine."

Linden's eyes rolled all the way up in their head, leaving only the vein-streaked whites to look at. Their entire body vibrated rapidly.

Urine made a dark, damp, acrid-smelling blotch on the crotch of their jeans.

River laughed.

Ash hummed.

Then, time disjointed completely. Sense smashed like a teacup against a moldy but still solid house wall. The world turned itself inside out for a while. River's guts turned themselves inside out. He was laughing, and then he was throwing up on the floor, again and again. Linden, still twitching, seemed to be unconscious. Some of his vomit splattered over them. Ash was wiping off Linden's face with the edge of a blanket. There were lines in the air all around them, like the auras Ash described sometimes. Layers and layers of skinny lines that rippled through translucent rainbow colors as they radiated outward. They moved with Ash. River blinked and blinked, but the lines didn't go away. He had to throw up again. The lines were making him nauseated—there was threat in their shimmer. The blue stained-glass speckles on the far wall screamed at him. Pain radiated up his spine, through his shoulders and hips. It branched into every part of him, like lightning. The blue was malevolent. The light was malevolent. River squeezed his eyes closed and fell on his hands and knees, and kept falling.

It was almost evening as he landed back in his skin. The blue had taken over. It was under Linden's skin—they lay still now, mouth still open, tongue still red, face sort of puffy and tinted with sky. The blue was in Ash's eyes and Ash was staring straight ahead, standing rigid and frozen like they had at the edge of the field a few days before. River looked at the undersides of his wrists and the blue was there too, squirming in fat snakes. But if he cut them open, he knew, they'd explode into red. How did that happen? The blue was the ghost of the teacups coming back for revenge from where their corpses had been ground into the yard's dry dirt. *Oh, Ash. You need to be more careful about what you destroy.*

But fire's never careful. It eats everything.

Dust clogged the room, entwining with those radiating lines in the air. Dust fell into Linden's open mouth. Dust fell into Ash's open eyes. River tried to avoid it, to shelter himself, but there was too much, and his limbs were too heavy, and they hurt. He was hot and cold at the same time. Red and blue at the same time. Red and blue and green and brown and. He looked at all the colors swimming through the world. Where were the angels?

Suddenly, Ash was gone. Light trails showed where they had wandered out the front door. River felt relieved, and he didn't know why. He was cold, so he went to Linden's side. Tried to give them an apology hug and snatch some body heat. But Linden was even colder.


An idea came to River in the form of a fish full of eyes that burst against his forehead. He wiped the drippings away and wanted to go upstairs. Then his legs unfolded beneath him. He moved very fast. He didn't perceive the movement. He was upstairs, holding the Instamatic. Downstairs was getting dark, but upstairs was darker. He wanted to go back down, and then there he was. Linden waited, tongue fuzzy with dust. River saw their face in more detail than he ever had before. The small scars on their earlobes where piercings had grown over. The scattering of wiry black hairs on their chin, and the way the hair on their upper lip was a mixture of black wires and chestnut down. Their eyelashes were stubby, but very thick. Caterpillar legs. River took a picture of Linden with the flash on. Linden didn't smile. Now he would always know what Linden looked like. Ash could know too, in the future, when they gave up their superstitions about photographs. Or maybe Ash would like a photograph of Linden, to control Linden as they might a video game character, a doll. Make Linden do whatever Ash wanted.


River tried to see the photo he'd taken, but he couldn't. The flash left too many swirling motes in the blue. Breaking up the blue, chasing it away, but blinding River in the process. Someone was singing.

"For to see Mad Tom of Bedlam, ten thousand miles I've traveled…"

River clutched the camera, trying to feel its heart through its smooth plastic sides. He imagined it was safe inside the camera, in the dark, where images could only appear in perfectly distilled, frozen, manageable chunks. Slices of world. River felt like the fish that had carried the idea of photography, like his body was full of too many eyes and they all just kept opening. The singing continued. It wasn't Linden, unless Linden's voice had gotten a lot higher all of a sudden and they'd learned to enunciate words with their mouth wide open and their tongue sticking out. Was it Ash? Where was Ash?

"Maudlin goes on dirty toes for to save his shoes from gravel! And it's well I sing, bonny boys, bonny mad boys—"

Was the voice River's own? It must have been. It followed him as he stumbled through the dark, taking the camera and its slick, still-developing spawn back upstairs. His body was slow again now, and his head felt too big. A helium balloon of a head, vast and full of terrible emptiness that wasn't empty at all when you zoomed in on it, but was made of billions of little sparks spinning and whizzing around, colliding…

"For they all go bare, and they live by the air, and they want no drink nor money!"

River curled against the porcelain of the bathtub, the porcelain of the tile. He fought off pain and nausea. He drifted up and out of his skin and through the moss-furred shingles of the roof.

Ash was calling River's name again. They didn't sound as angry or sad or panicked as they had the night they'd struck his face and he'd run off into the woods, but they did sound pensive. Worried. And their voice was awfully loud. River wrenched his eyes a little way open, so that they were just tiny slits against the morning sun. Even in the dim, windowless bathroom, it seemed obscenely bright. His head was a bowling ball full of needles. He sat up in a series of tentative jolts, wincing as his spine popped.

The camera lay on the floor beside him, and when he looked down at his hands, he realized he was still clutching the photo he'd taken. He examined it through his pained squint. Linden's face, with tongue protruding, was pale and washed out from the flash. It appeared to float alone in darkness. Linden beheaded. Linden's mouth too wide and too red. All the hairs, acne scars, and small, fine lines on their skin had been erased by the brightness. This gave their features an eerie, mask-like quality that added to the ghoulishness. River shuddered. He shoved the camera back in its place beneath the tub, and slipped the photo into the breast pocket of his army jacket when he put it on. Triple-checked to make sure that the pocket flap was buttoned before he made his way downstairs. His thoughts felt slow and erratic. There was something off about the world's colors, the speed at which sound traveled.

"River!" called Ash. "River, get down here! I need some assistance!" River tried to move faster, but succeeded only in lurching forward and falling down the last few stairs. He caught himself, but the floor smacked into his palms so hard, he was sure they'd bruise.

"Good," Ash's voice said. "You're awake. Now stop fooling around." After some disoriented confusion, River determined that Ash was in the room of the Auspicious Window.

Linden was, too. River stepped across the threshold and froze. There was a faint piss and shit smell in the air. Linden's face still looked blue-tinged and puffy, like they'd choked or drowned. Their mouth and eyes drooped open. Their tongue still lolled out. Their limbs were stiff and unyielding—River could tell, because Ash was struggling mightily to get Linden's clothes off. They'd managed the urine-soaked jeans and boxer shorts, but their shirt was giving them problems. Linden's arms stubbornly refused to rise.

"You might have to cut their shirt off, Ash." River sounded much calmer than he felt. "I don't think you can get their arms up. It's rigor mortis."

"That's what I was thinking," Ash grunted, not missing a beat. "I've got a pair of scissors in my room. Will you go up and get them for me?"

River hesitated. "Ash, why are you taking Linden's clothes off? We should bury them or something, right? They don't have to be naked for that. It's probably more respectful if they aren't." *How are you so calm?* he screamed at himself inside his head. *I know you hated Linden, but you're not a bad person! You should be horrified by this! Devastated!*

River shook his head to get rid of his conscience's slavering panic. It wouldn't help anything. The entire situation still felt like a dream, or a TV show. Like it wasn't really him here in the room helping Ash at all, and it wasn't Ash trying to strip a corpse, and it wasn't Linden lying there on the black sheet, the dark cotton now heavily streaked and splotched with all kinds of bodily fluids.

"Why would we abandon Linden?" Ash sounded shocked and affronted. "Let alone bury them? Really, River. I thought you'd know better. Linden will be fine. I'm just trying to get them back into their ceremonial robe before we put them somewhere to rest until—"

"They don't need *rest*, Ash!"

Ash looked pitying. "*River.* Linden is one of us, a holy elemental vessel, part of the body of God. Linden can't *die*. Not permanently. This is the outcome of their test: they did not fail, but they must continue with their human body in a state of suspension until the vessel of air finds its way to us and the final days arrive." Ash paused for a moment, thoughtful. "We should put them in the bathtub. The porcelain and the animal feet are very regal. It's befitting. You won't mind sleeping with me, will you, River?"

"No," said River. Of course he didn't mind. *But you never wanted it like this, did you? Or did you?*

"Good. Fetch me my scissors and Linden's robe. Move your things out of the bathroom. When you've done that, we'll carry the vessel of earth upstairs." They let go of Linden carefully, then sat down beside the body, looking vacant. Twisted the largest ring on their fingers around and around, until River thought the finger itself might pop off, unscrewed.

"What are you going to do?" he asked Ash.

"I'll be out picking flowers." Ash began to hum to themself. The sound followed River back upstairs as a maddening whine that he could almost see hanging in the air before him. Like static on an old TV set. He thought he could feel the photograph of Linden rustling against his chest through his jacket.

**II.** Ash and River had to burn the black sheets. Ash made a pyre outside and cut the sheets into strips for faster incineration. Linden's shirt, socks, boxers, jeans, and shoes went on the fire too. The shoes didn't burn right, they just turned charred and misshapen. River suggested that they bury the shoes instead, and Ash didn't object.

Before they burned the sheets and buried the shoes, they stripped Linden down to their binder (River scratched where his own armpit chafed beneath his double-layered sports bras and envied how perfectly flat it made Linden's chest). Ash wrangled Linden into their coarse, too-small brown robe. Lifted Linden's shoulders and River lifted Linden's feet, and together, they carried the body upstairs to the bathtub. River looked at their toes to avoid thinking about anything much. Linden's toes were short and square—tipped, curled like cashews, with a fine dusting of hair on their knuckles and the kind of nails that curved concave instead of convex, forming odd little dips. Slits in the flesh.

Ash had some difficulty making Linden fit in the tub—their stiff legs splayed out too long. Finally, with a sickening crack, they managed to bend Linden into a stooped, unnatural half-sit that allowed their body to recline in the bathtub, their arms slightly elevated at odd angles and their head bent down towards their chest. Their fingers seemed to claw at the tub's chipped white rim.

River's hand went nervously to his breast pocket, where the Linden in the photograph screamed silently in the dark. His vision blurred, and he found himself needing to sit down on the floor so he wouldn't fall.

"That's good," said Ash. "You two rest here." They went to fetch the armfuls of flowers they'd gathered, garlanded. As if even in the dimness of the upstairs bathroom, they wanted their colors to shine out at a visitor like the eyes of angels.

Linden sat in the bathtub and did not move. A cockroach found its way into the tub and crawled across Linden's lap, then up their chest. Onto their face. It rested for some time in the moist cave of their open mouth before departing for the summit of their prickly close-shorn hair. Linden had not brought their phone with them to the house, or their wallet, or anything especially identifying. Dimly, River knew that this was good. Lucky. Linden had had a twenty dollar bill shoved in the back pocket of their jeans, and River dimly knew that this was good and lucky too. Before they'd burned the clothes, he'd slipped the money into his own jacket pocket almost reflexively, without telling Ash about it. He worried his friend might insist that they allow Linden to keep the bill, or insist that they burn it along with Linden's clothes. But River knew that they were going to need that twenty dollars for something sooner or later, and that Linden would never need money again.

After the fire was nothing but a circle of stones and smoldering black-burned branches in a clear patch of dirt near the edge of the trees, after the shoes were under a foot of earth and a heavy rock, after Linden's body had been crowned, piled, surrounded with flowers, Ash lay back in the long grass and stared up at the sky. Dark gray clouds were rolling over its blue, slowly and steadily and silently.

"It's going to rain," said Ash.

"That's good, right? We haven't had a real spring rain yet." River peered down at Ash's face. They looked worn, vacant again. Their voice had a flat, empty sound that River wasn't accustomed to. He looked away. The trees were getting greener and greener. River heard the whine of a mosquito, but couldn't spot the bug.

"Ash?" he asked. "What's wrong?" *What do you think is wrong?* his conscience snarled at him.

"I can't hear the angels anymore. I don't understand why not. They've never left me before. I haven't heard them much since last night, or at all since the fire burned out."

River didn't know what to say, so he stayed silent.

"I've always done what they wanted me to do," Ash continued. "I've always relied on them for guidance."

"Maybe... maybe they want you to make your own decisions from now on?" River hedged.

"No." Ash shook their head emphatically, tangling dirt and fallen leaves in their curls. "This vessel isn't worthy to make decisions. Not as it is. That's too much responsibility."

"Well, maybe the angels will come back."

"I hope so." Ash sighed. "Everything's so close to perfect now. I can taste the final days already."


The storm clouds gathered and hung low above the treetops and rooftops like distended animal teats. They rumbled. They cracked with veins and branches of electricity. They burst with rain, and the rain fell all through the evening and the night and the morning of the next day.

Rain drummed like dropped coins on the roof above the bedroom where Ash lay spooning River, chaste but intimate as two siblings. Ash's skinny arms gripped painfully tight around River's belly, and he lay sleepless all through the storm but never moved. He thought he could hear whispering in his ear where it was pillowed on his folded-up jacket. Not the voice of his conscience, and not Ash's angels. Linden's voice, far away and mixed with thunder. Linden's voice trickling out of the hole that was their open throat in the photograph, haunting him. "Bedlam boys are bonny..."

Rain splattered like spit and tears on the roof above the bathroom where Linden rotted in an old bathtub, covered in flowers that were rotting too. Linden stared sightlessly at brown plaid and yellow petals, shiny dark insect backs. They had already begun to bloat a little in the warm, damp weather, their skin turning doughy and greenish, inflating.

When it was no longer night, but still raining, Ash came and sat with Linden for a few minutes. They tried to hold Linden's hand, but quickly thought better of it. They spoke to the corpse for hours, but Linden did not hear them and did not respond to them, and finally, the flowery, farty smell of the room, just beginning to edge over into rank decay, drove Ash away.

The rain had stopped, and the world outside was still soaking wet. The sunlight was weak and halfhearted. Ash had brought a bottle-candle into the bathroom— when they left, the candle stayed. Wax pooled on the tile.

## Corrupted Vessels

After a little more time, River came into the bathroom, bags under his eyes, looking more fifty than fifteen, breathing heavy through his open mouth and pinching his nose shut with one hand. He stood staring at Linden for a minute. He mumbled irritable remarks—not to the corpse, but to some entity only he could hear. Pinched out the candle with the bare fingertips of his free hand, not reacting to the burn at all, and carried the bottle out with him, shutting the bathroom door firmly as he left.

A new cockroach crawled up Linden's swollen tongue, into their mouth. This one liked it there, and decided to stay for a while. Time slid forward, as time will. Once, twice, three times the sky grew pale and bright, then fiery at sunset, then dark and dotted with stars like glowing animal eyes. Coyotes snuffled around outside the house in the woods. Linden swelled and stank. The seams of their robe and binder unraveled in places and threatened to burst. Fluid leaked from their mouth. Flies laid their eggs in all of Linden's orifices and landed on the collapsing blossoms of jessamine and butterwort and lupine. The flies rubbed their bristly arms together and watched impassively through compound eyes as fluid dripped from Linden's nose and mouth and eye sockets. As their skin began to split like an overripe peach.

The bathroom door stayed shut. At some point, if Linden had still been able to hear, they would have heard the pounding of hammer and nails on the other side. If they'd been able to see, they would have watched the walls shake and shed great clots of plaster as they were sealed into their porcelain tomb.

The bugs and vermin hardly noticed, or cared.

There were always plenty of cracks and holes for them to travel through.

They'd had a week of sunny, warm weather, but now the spring storms were back again, and they weren't letting up. The smell inside the house had gotten so bad that River and Ash had begun spending all their time outdoors, even sleeping in the branches of trees at night or lying in the long grass together during the day, then roaming awake through the dark hours. This afternoon, lightning and heavy rain had forced them back inside, and the only thing for it was to burn incense and try to breathe only through their mouths. They stayed inside the room of the Auspicious Window and placed a waste bucket in the far corner of the living room. By mutual unspoken agreement, the second floor of the house was now off limits.

River thought with regret of the paperback novels he'd left up there, and with even more regret of the camera, and his Book. Now, the only thing he had to occupy his time outside of Ash's conversation was—

"You *could* go up there, you know," said Linden's voice, archly, from his pocket.

"Shhh!" River hissed.

Ash, still unable to hear the angels, still in a funk, didn't seem to notice that River had been acting strangely over the past several days, talking back to something hidden in the recesses of his jacket.

Right now, Ash was sitting motionless on bent knees before the altar, palms turned upward in their lap. Their eyes were open and blank. They hummed and hummed, tuneless, maddening, extremely out of it. Nonetheless, River didn't want to take chances. He believed Ash remained capable of wrath, and finding out about the photograph he'd taken (stolen) as Linden lay dying (poisoned) would surely rouse their anger. They might even blame River for the smell, for the inescapable fact of Linden's decay. Ash might tell River that he was the true murderer here. That if he hadn't captured Linden's soul on film, their body would have stayed fresh and incorruptible until the time came for them to awaken and take their place beside the vessels of fire, water, and air.

Maybe Ash would even be right. Maybe River was a monster. *No.* River shook his head to clear it of the thought. He was being stupid. The voice in his pocket wasn't real. It was like the heart under the floorboards in that story he'd read once, a manifestation of his guilt. A residual effect of whatever'd been in his drink that fatal night. He didn't believe he was a mystic or a prophet, and anyway, a ghost was not an angel. River didn't really believe in ghosts, either. That left hallucination.

"Sure, kid," said Linden. "You keep on telling yourself that."

*If you can hear my thoughts,* River thought fiercely at the unseen, masklike face in the photograph, *that just proves I made you up. You're a part of me, not something that exists outside in the world.*

"Things inside you are just as real as things outside you, most of the time," Linden observed. "Anyway, I'm a dead guy talking to you from a picture. I don't think it would be that surprising if I were also telepathic, do you? Why would normal conversational rules even apply here? It doesn't prove *shit*."

River's stomach growled. He considered opening his and Ash's last can of Spaghetti-O's, and eating them cold with the plastic sporks he'd stolen from a McDonald's. No, he should make Ash eat first. They no longer ate or drank anything if River didn't push it on them. River felt himself flush and burn with a potent mix of fear and tenderness and guilt, remembering how it had taken almost two days after they'd put Linden's body in the tub for him to notice. Ash had fainted at the edge of the woods, crushing an anthill. Ants bit them all over one shoulder as they lay collapsed for several minutes in a mess of churned mud and grass. River had been so terrified that Ash, too, had died and left him all alone again.

"Go ahead," Linden said kindly. "It'll stop raining tomorrow, and you've got most of that twenty bucks left. You can buy some decent food, for once. It's just too bad I can't still bring by sandwiches."

*You don't know when it'll stop raining,* thought River, but he was already walking into the kitchen, opening the cupboard where they kept their food, drinks, dishes, and utensils. He retrieved the Spaghetti-O's, two sporks, and a mostly empty bottle of Diet Mountain Dew. He ran his hand across the back of the cupboard shelves, hopefully. Two other soda bottles, soda long drained, re-filled with water from the fountain at the public library. Unused Solo cups from the pack Ash had gotten for their ritual. A dead roach. A vending machine packet of peanut butter crackers, unopened. That was all, and River was sure they all smelled like... *well*. He wondered if simply being in the same house as a poisoned dead body could contaminate things. Make them unfit for human consumption.

## Corrupted Vessels

He wished the rain would ease up a little. If it did, he'd go raid the bakery's dumpster, which had a busted lock. He'd use Linden's money to buy burgers for himself and Ash. Anything but this. A huge baroom! of thunder made the dead roach jump on its back, its carapace sliding against the peanut butter cracker packet. River jumped a little too.

"The weather's the weather," Linden told him. "There's no helping it. And I told you, it'll let up tomorrow. While you're stuck in here, I think you oughta tell Ash who you saw in the field yesterday. Watching the house."

*Who did I see?* Then he remembered. Yesterday, walking among the trees at the edge of the clearing, River had noticed a figure standing on the opposite side, toward the east of the house instead of the west, just outside the tree line. He knew at once that it wasn't Ash. This person was shorter and fat—not just soft and a little doughy, like River, but huge, strong and very solid-looking. The person had dark skin, and darker hair and clothes. Silver jewelry glinted in their ears and nose. Their hands were on their hips and their feet were planted far apart. They were watching the house, not hiding, but quiet and still. Wary. River wasn't sure, but he thought the person was frowning—frowning so deeply that he could see it from all the way on the other side of the field.

River watched the person for a while, and eventually, they left, melting back into the shadows between trees. Presumably headed for the footpath that led into town.

The experience had left River unsettled. He'd told

himself it was nothing, a coincidence. It was ridiculous to expect that no one except him, Ash, and Linden would ever find the clearing and the house. It was far off the trail, but not that far, and not hard to reach at all. People wandered, people hiked. Probably people stumbled into the long grass and wildflowers every week, looked curiously across the field at the decaying house for a few minutes, and left, never to return or think about it again.

"Nah," said Linden. "They don't. She was *searching*. She'll be back."

"Searching for who? You?" River whispered out loud. He realized what he was doing and felt instantly foolish, but the words were already out there in the damp, stagnant air of the kitchen, mixing with the heavy sweet stink.

"Yes, searching for me. That was my friend. My ex-girlfriend, even... well, she wouldn't want me to call her that. We had our differences. But she's worried about me. She suspects something really bad happened."

*I don't know who it was,* River thought. *So you don't, either. That could've been anybody.* It was a halfhearted argument.

"I'm just trying to warn you, kid," said Linden. "You two may have killed me, but I'd hate to see you go to jail. Not like that'd bring me back. And we had some good times, didn't we?" Their voice was wistful.

River brought the Spaghetti-O's into the room of the Auspicious Window, thinking: *Shut up.*

"Ash? I have dinner," he said aloud. "Ash, you need to eat something."

"Tell Ash about my girlfriend," insisted Linden. "Watching us. Tell them about her."

## Corrupted Vessels

*Shut up*, thought River. *Just shut the fuck up, you stupid haunting.*

"I'm not hungry," muttered Ash, but they took the spork and the can when River pushed them into Ash's ring-adorned hands.

III. Nora sat in a wide, battered wooden chair on the front porch of Bug House and joylessly smoked her fifth cigarette in a row. Most of the time she kept it down to three or four a day and never chain-smoked. She couldn't bring herself to feel guilty about this lapse, but she wrinkled her nose and coughed as she thumbed through Linden's abandoned phone, looking for something, *anything*, that might help her solve the mystery of her friend and sometime-lover's disappearance.

Nora tapped out her cigarette's long pillar of ash in a carnival glass tray perched precariously on the porch's front railing. Jamal loped out the front door, letting it slam behind him.

"'Sup?" He nodded at Nora.

"Not much, man."

"Linden still AWOL, I take it?"

"Yeah."

"Cops still useless?"

"Obviously. They're cops." Nora sighed. "They said Linden's an adult. There are no signs of foul play. They'll keep an eye out, but there's no reason to think Linden hasn't just gone off on a weeklong bender somewhere, or decided to skip town for personal reasons. Which is 100% legal."

"Linden doesn't do benders. And they left without their wallet and phone! Who does that, if they mean to be gone for more than a couple hours?"

"I know, Jamal. I know. Look, I'll try the cops again soon. I'm not optimistic, but I'll try."

"Good luck." Jamal started down the front steps, his hands jammed in the pockets of his cargo shorts. He turned back for a moment when he reached the beginning of the front walk. "You contact Linden's parents yet?"

"Yeah. They're worried. Coming down here as soon as they can get time off work and arrange to travel."

"Maybe *they'll* have better luck with the police."

"Maybe. See you, Jamal."

Jamal gave Nora a jaunty tip of his newsboy cap and strode purposefully away down the sidewalk. Nora took a long drag on her cigarette and studied the phone screen.

It hadn't been hard to get into Linden's phone. The passcode was just their birthday (08-30-98). Nora had been elated when she found the phone, lying in plain sight on Linden's desk. No snooping through Linden's messy room required. She was sure that the answer to Linden's disappearance lay within. When she'd first unlocked the phone, more than five days earlier, Nora had expected to learn sad, frightening news about her friend's probable fate. She had already crafted several vivid scenarios in her mind's eye over the past few sleepless nights, most of them variations on a drug deal gone wrong or an overdose. Sure, Linden had sworn up and down for a month that they weren't doing drugs, but Nora had seen this story play out before in other members of their friend group, in people she knew back home. She wasn't naive. She knew what uncharacteristic secrecy, behavioral changes, erratic moods, lapsed focus, sudden lack of spare cash to go out at night, and all the rest of Linden's symptoms were likely to mean.

But there was nothing amiss on Linden's phone. They hadn't been posting on social media as frequently, but they had been posting. Their text messages seemed normal, contained nothing cryptic and nothing Nora thought might be a code. There were no conversations with people whose names Nora didn't recognize, no repeated calls to strange phone numbers. Of course, it was always possible that Linden had been smart, had been more careful and disciplined than usual, and had exclusively used a burner phone for everything. It would be surprising behavior from a person who used their birthday as a password and routinely forgot to lock the front door at night, God love them.

But it was always *possible*.

Nora sighed again, and she felt tears gathering in her lower eyelids, stinging her, trembling on her lashes. Whether the tears came from frustration, from smoke irritation, or from something much deeper and worse, she didn't know.

It was an Easter egg painting of a spring day. Birds sang cheerfully in the trees, in the eaves of houses. Nora could hear children screeching and laughing and bouncing balls down the block. She put the phone down on the porch rail next to the ashtray and stubbed out the last nub of her cigarette. She leaned forward and put her head in her hands. The chair creaked beneath her. Her shoulders ached with tension. Jesus Christ, she was so tired. She was so goddamn *tired*—of worrying, of losing friends, of being the only person who cared enough to be responsible, to be diligent, to be concerned.

She was tired of everything.

Tired of *life*.

Nora wept quietly into her palms. Then she leaned back and fell asleep right there, slumped in the uncomfortable wooden chair, legs stretched out before her, rumpled black dress dusted with ash and smelling of carcinogens.

Nora dreamed.

In the dream, Nora was in Linden's body. Light skin, stubble-hair, corded muscle, much thinner than she'd ever been. When she scratched her chin, there were bristles there. She had become Linden, and Linden was in a forest.

At first, it was a northern forest of tall pines and chattering squirrels and deep, dry shadows dusted with the glimmer of snow. A fairy tale forest, the kind of forest Nora remembered from school vacations visiting her stepmother's extended family in Maine as a child. Now, everything she saw was from a child's eye view, although Linden wasn't short. The trees loomed the way they had when she was eight years old, their lowest branches still high above her head. The trees seemed to go on forever. Dead needles and leaves crunched beneath her feet—Linden's feet—as she began to walk. She moved down a narrow, ill-defined path, and heard whispering all around her.

*It's only the wind,* Nora told herself, knowing that it wasn't. There was a wind blowing though, a warm wind, and it seemed to push her forward. The colors of the landscape warped and melted together as the wind rushed over them, and the forest became a different forest. The earth grew damp and muddy. Small lizards scuttled across the path. Spanish moss drooped from the branches of live oaks. The world grew smaller, or she grew taller, and her perspective was no longer a child's, but she was still Linden, now restored to Linden's proper height. It made her feel stretched like a piece of gum, too long and narrow.

She recognized the new woods, too. Nora didn't enjoy taking nature walks in the South, which was too humid and swampy. Too full of mosquitoes. Full of plants that made her cough and wheeze when she'd never had allergies before in her life. But she had used this shortcut through the patch of forest that oozed into the center of town like an abscess. Linden had shown it to her when they'd first met, before she'd bought her car.

Now, Nora heard a voice singing—Linden's voice, reverberating in an unfamiliar way now that she was inside Linden's skull. Nora did not want to sing, but she seemed to be a passenger here, not a driver. She felt her throat work as the words poured lustily forth in Linden's awkward, breaking tenor. It was one of those morbid white people folk songs Linden liked to sing whenever they were doing the Bug House dishes.

"My staff has murdered giants, my pack the long knife carries—to cut mince pies from children's thighs with which to feed the fairies! And it's well I sing, bonny boys, bonny mad boys..."

Nora had no problem with morbidity, but under the circumstances, she wished Linden would sing something else. A terrible foreboding was growing inside her, and she wished with all her might that Linden would turn around, would leave the woods, would obey her frantic instructions to Linden's legs and arms and mouth, would please, please, please sing something else.

Instead, Linden turned off the path, pushing aside branches and tatters of hanging moss and vines. They headed deeper into the woods, still singing. Soon, the brush was so thick around them that it was hard to see more than a few feet in any direction. Invisible animals, birds, and insects rustled, chirped, and hummed. It was still broad daylight, and not too dark even among the deep green shadows of the trees. There was no obvious danger here. All the same, Nora's terror grew—had she been in her own body, or able to control Linden's, she would have run for the path. Maybe cried, or even screamed.

Linden pressed through a dense thicket of bushes. Nora felt thorns scratch her bare arms, Linden didn't seem to care. Then, abruptly, they were in a clearing. It was full of tall grass and scattered wildflowers or weeds Nora couldn't name. The weeds bent in the wind like the bodies of lovers, like fine, dense hair. The sky was high and nearly colorless above the field. Nora couldn't find the sun in it. In the middle of the clearing was a tall, dark pillar of roiling smoke. It looked filthy, sinister, something poisonous spewed out of a factory chimney. Something that would choke rivers into sludgy quicksand and give babies birth defects. It reached up and up into the colorless sky, stretching far above the highest treetops before it finally tapered out. An evil, oily, meaty smell hung in the air, and the incomprehensible whispering had returned, oppressively loud, coming from all sides and from no source that Nora could discern.

Linden stopped and stood just inside the clearing. Wheatish grass heads brushed their hips. Linden wasn't singing anymore. They extended their arm and pointed straight ahead, right at the smoky pillar.

"Do you see that?" Linden's voice was still so strange

to hear from the inside. Nora could feel the dryness of Linden's lips, the slick wetness of tongue against teeth, the fuzz at the back of their mouth where they hadn't brushed very well. Nora could taste Linden's sour spit welling up as they spoke. She wanted to scream. She wanted to scream so badly.

"That's what happened to me," they said, matter-of-factly.

Nora startled awake with a gasp and a shudder, almost flinging herself out of the chair she'd fallen asleep in. She had never experienced this kind of abrupt ejection from a nightmare before. When she'd read about it in books or seen it in movies, she'd always assumed it was just a dramatic device. Her heart was pounding and her armpits were soaked in sweat.

"Jesus fucking Christ," Nora muttered. Shaking, she found her purse resting underneath the chair where she'd left it. Fished out her pack of cigarettes and her lighter. Time for Smoke Number Six, lung cancer be damned.

It was almost evening. The sunset was gory and gorgeous. Nora watched it melt from gold to hot pink as she smoked, from hot pink to a red as vivid as the cherry at the end of her cigarette. She must have been dozing for at least a couple of hours. God, she had to get a really good night's rest, and soon.

Nora took a last cursory scroll through Linden's text messages, but her mind was on her dream. She didn't believe in ghosts, or psychic powers, or premonitions, or any of that stuff, but she didn't not believe in them either. The phone certainly wasn't yielding up any answers. Linden's parents wouldn't arrive in town for a few days, and Nora really didn't relish the prospect of talking to the cops again, especially by herself, and especially with no new information. The dream had had a clear message. Even if it was nothing but the confused, dead-end babbling of her troubled subconscious, it wouldn't hurt to go out to the woods tomorrow and look around. She'd tell friends when to expect her home, and she'd bring her phone... and she knew she could handle herself in a physical fight, if it came down to it. She'd be fine.

It would be nothing. The woods would contain no mysterious clearing, no answers for her. She would have wasted an afternoon she could have spent catching up on homework she'd missed over the past week-and-change of obsessing over Linden's disappearance.

She'd be fine, and it would be nothing. But she owed it to Linden to follow any and every potential lead, no matter how crazy or stupid or unlikely. She had to go and look.


There *was* a clearing, just as she'd dreamed it.

Nora felt a cold sweat break out on her forehead, distinct in odor and tactile sensation from the hot, soupy sweat she'd worked up traipsing around the woods in an outfit that, like almost all of Nora's outfits, was never intended for vigorous physical activity in warm weather. To calm her nerves, she rebuked herself for not digging her one pair of practical athletic shorts out of the dresser, much as she hated to wear them. Oh, well. Too late now.

Pink flowers swirled in a slight, moist breeze, and the ragged edges of tall grass stalks made Nora's hands itch. A frog croaked loudly nearby. It was a pretty day, though Nora could tell from the smell in the air that the spring rains would soon return. All this, though, was backdrop.

No pillar of rancid smoke writhed toward heaven in the middle of the clearing. But there was a house there, rising like an island from the lake of grass. It was a two-story Victorian-looking affair, like many of the older houses in town. Nora couldn't figure out how it had gotten here. The building was decrepit, probably abandoned for years or decades. Nora could tell that, even from a distance. It slumped into itself like a tired old man, spotted with mold, fungus, moss, and lichen. Paint peeled from its sides like skin tags. Each window was a dark, empty hole, unless it was boarded up.

It gave Nora the creeps. More, even, than the fact of her dream-clearing's existence in the waking world. A smell drifted toward her from the house, a half sour, half sick-sweet odor of decay, like the time an opossum had died in the back of Bug House's garage and nobody had been able to find the corpse for two weeks. Nora couldn't shake the feeling that someone was watching her, silent, intent, and invisible. Someone who did not like that she had come here.

Nora tried to feel brave and confident. She took a step in the direction of the house. She would explore it. She should explore it, for Linden's sake. But what if...?

*What if you don't want to find out what's inside?*

Nora gritted her teeth. She wasn't a coward. She didn't believe that not knowing a painful truth was ever preferable to discovering and dealing with it. She didn't believe in ghosts and she didn't believe in premonitions either. Linden must have mentioned this place to her at some point in the past. She'd mostly forgotten about it, but her brain had dredged it up from the recesses of her memory while she'd slept.

The powerful sensation of being watched? Her imagination. Or an animal, a coyote prowling around in the bushes. Or something to do with the Earth's electromagnetic field, like she'd read about in an article on those ghost-hunting TV shows one time.

Nora was going into that house. She would explore it here and now. It wasn't a big deal and it wouldn't take very long. She might find nothing. She might find something tragic. Either way, she was in no danger. She'd handle it, the same way she handled everything else in her life.

Something snapped loudly across the clearing. Something rustled in the bushes at the tree line.

Nora froze and squinted. She saw a human figure moving, weaving between shadows, trying to hide. They were successful enough that she couldn't make out anything about them: not their age, gender, race, size. But they walked on two feet for sure, and they were wearing clothes.

Nora stood still and thought for a moment, calculating.

The best course of action, she decided, would be to return and explore the house later, at a different time of day. Maybe early in the morning, when it was less likely that anyone else would come snooping around. For now, she'd act uninterested. She'd give no sign that she'd seen the figure in the bushes, and she'd leave.

Maybe that was silly, over-cautious. Well, so what. The house would wait.

Nora turned her back on the ominous ruin and made her strategic retreat. She refused to admit to herself that she felt eyes staring at her back, that she imagined breath on her neck and fingers reaching out to scrape her spine the whole way into town.

The next day it rained from before dawn until after midnight. Nora spent most of that time in Linden's room, searching through Linden's belongings with only minimal guilt. She found some print copies of furry porn comics (Linden was into that stuff?), a couple of vibrators, a skull-shaped bong she was already quite familiar with, and a Baggie of weed. She found Linden's testosterone and needles. She found an orange plastic bottle of small candy-blue pills whose label identified them as a generic brand substitute for Adderall. For a moment, Nora thought this offered strong evidence in favor of her theory that Linden had a secret drug problem. True, Adderall was hardly heroin or meth, but... Nora's train of thought came to a whimpering halt as she read the rest of the label. The medication had been prescribed to Linden by one of the university doctors months earlier. Not only had Linden gotten the meds by legitimate means, the number of pills left in the bottle indicated that they'd only been taking them sporadically, if at all. Nothing else in Linden's room pointed towards drug use, a secret life, or anything remotely unusual. Nora felt a combination of frustration, relief, and, above all, confusion.

It just didn't make sense.

She sat in a nest of her vanished friend's dirty laundry and loose school papers, breathing in Linden's boy-puberty-and-cheap-cologne smell. Objectively it wasn't a great smell, but it belonged to someone she loved. Rain clattered on Bug House's roof like fistfuls of pebbles. Laughter and talk wafted up from the kitchen and living room downstairs, and Nora admitted to herself that Linden was probably dead. One way or another.

Nora cried. She considered smoking Linden's weed, but decided against it. She put everything back where she'd found it. Curled up on Linden's mattress, right on top of the slight indentation where Linden habitually lay.

She slept.

Again, Nora dreamed.

Linden was fucking her against a wall in a place she'd never been. Their tongue ran over every ridge of Nora's teeth, and their hands kneaded her flesh like dough. Nora trembled and groaned. The wall under her back felt spongey and shaggy with flaking wallpaper. It was dim and dusty. Wooden floorboards. A staircase dropped down to a heavy closed door behind Linden's naked shoulders.

"Should we be here?" asked Nora, when her mouth was uncovered and she had enough breath for it. "Someone could see us. Someone could catch us."

She didn't know who she meant, exactly, but she felt a house potentially filled with eyes and ears spreading around them, hushed and waiting.

It scared her, and it turned her on.

She raked her nails across Linden's hips and pulled them closer. They were finding a fast, hard rhythm together. It was urgent sex, almost rushed. They needed to finish soon, before someone (but who?) walked in the door at the bottom of the stairs and found them tangled together like this.

"Shh," Linden whispered into Nora's ear. "Pay attention. This is the place. There's a door behind you, to your left. At the top of the stairs. Say it."

"Top of the stairs?"

"That's the place."

Nora rocked and shuddered. "Linden..."

"Say it. That's the place. Promise me you'll go."

Nora felt the frustrating itch of an orgasm building.

"Linden, baby, please..." she said.

"This is the place. At the top of the stairs." Linden's hands froze. Their body stiffened, cooled. "Did you hear that?"

"No," said Nora, but she was lying. She heard the creaking of the door beginning to open. She saw it start to push out from its frame over Linden's shoulder. A tall shadow wavered there. Someone was about to step through. There was no time to hide.

"This is the place," Linden whispered again, voice distorted. Their eyes were wide. Bright red liquid had begun to bubble up from the back of their throat. "This is the place. Promise."

Someone was stepping through the door, but Nora still couldn't see anything but their shadow. Nora couldn't hear anyone breathing.

She couldn't breathe. She—

Nora woke up stifling a scream. She sucked air from the darkness in huge, desperate gulps, trying to figure out where she was. Not in her room, not in her bed. The ceiling wasn't right, nor the firmness and slant of the mattress beneath her.

The folds of flesh at her waist felt sore and irritated, uncomfortably constrained. She explored the area with her hand, found the waistband of her skirt over the waistband of her tights. God. Why had she fallen asleep in her clothes? How had she fallen asleep in her clothes? She felt like her middle was in the process of being squeezed through a snake's digestive tract.

Everything came back to her in a rush. Linden's room. Of course. She'd been crying. Of course. She hadn't had a good night's sleep in so long she probably could have nodded off almost anywhere, no matter what she was wearing. Nora remembered the house in the field, and her plan to return when the rain had stopped. *Tomorrow? The day after tomorrow? Today? What time is it?*

She remembered the flaking paint on the outside of the house. She remembered the peeling wallpaper in the hallway she'd dreamed. *This is the place.*

Nora reminded herself, very, very firmly, that she didn't believe in ghosts, or premonitions, or psychic powers. Her dream meant that she was horny and scared and grieving, spooked by an abandoned building and a figure she'd barely glimpsed at the edge of the woods. That was all. She would go back as soon as she could and prove it to herself.

*Promise?*


And at the next clear dawn, Nora made her way into the woods again. The rising sun streaked the sky hot pink and lavender behind her. The shadows of the trees were almost indigo and smelled of wet fur. She worried for a moment that it might be too dark for her to see where she was going, but as morning brightened the world, her eyes adjusted to the gloom. The indigo turned to a palette of greens and grays and browns. Squirrels and lizards began their scampering quests for food. Songbirds propositioned one another from on high, and Nora knew exactly where to go. Though she had only visited the clearing once before—twice, if you counted her dream on the front porch of Bug House—the route from forest edge to field of tall grass and collapsing ruin was burned into her memory, stuck there like an especially tenacious scrap of pop music.

Her boots stomped through mud and thorny weeds. She pushed aside spiderwebs and Spanish moss and the whip-thin bodies of inconveniently positioned saplings. She parted a curtain of leaves and needles, still beaded with rain from the previous day. And there was the sea of long grass and wildflowers. There was the house like an abandoned, slowly sinking ship. The sky was a huge, high bowl above the clearing, pale blue streaked with irritated scratches of magenta.

Today there was no breeze to blow any smells towards Nora. The air was still and damp and close. All the same, that sour-sweet stench she'd noticed the other day hit her nose when she was yet a good distance from the house. It only got more powerful as she approached the dilapidated, mold-wrecked porch. The front door. Nora gagged, but she forced herself to continue. She breathed through her mouth, even pinching her nostrils closed between her thumb and forefinger like a child miming

"P.U." The door was shedding paint. It stuck out from the jamb a little, swollen. Its knob was red-orange, lumpy, rusted. Nora turned it with a firm, squeaking twist and push-pulled the door until it yielded to her assault. She stepped over the threshold.

Flies drifted lazily through the dim air inside the house. There was a haze, a miasma like that rotting smell made visible, like the air itself was rotting. Nora pinched her nose shut again.

To one side of her, a short hallway led to what looked like a kitchen, with a tile floor and a sink filled with browning plants. (Nora hoped the plants were the source of the smell, and knew that they weren't.) To the other side, an ugly, plush armchair sat on the floorboards of what might've once been a parlor or living room, the only surviving furniture there. Its back played host to extravagant fungal growth, shelf on shelf of gilled and seeping things clamoring to overtake the summit of the chair and spill over to its front and arms. Two dark glass bottles crusted with wax stood beside the armchair, candle stubs protruding from their mouths.

In front of Nora, the staircase ascended, just as she'd dreamed it. Plain, not too tall. Walls on either side, one with a slim, broken banister railing inset. Some of the stairs slanted a little, uneven with time and neglect. Nora took a deep mouth-breath. She clenched her free hand into a fist. Then, as slowly and as quietly as she could, she started climbing the stairs. She knew there was no need for stealth. No one else was here. No one could be here. Even if the house had been used as a squat or a place to shoot up in the recent past, it wouldn't be tolerable to linger for any length of time now, with the stench and the flies. Surely, it wouldn't. The place was silent but for the buzzing and clicking of insects. A grave-silence, a death-silence. There was no need for stealth, but Nora winced and froze for a moment—every time the stairs creaked under her weight, every time her footfalls made noise. She noticed that the stairs weren't covered in thick dust, as she might have expected. That disturbed her. Her dream kept returning to echo around in her mind's eye and ear. These same stairs, from another perspective. The shadow at the door. *This is the place.*

Nora stepped into the too-familiar hall at the top of the staircase. There was a door at one end, cracked slightly open. It seemed to lead into a bedroom. At the other end of the hall, a tall, narrow window leaked murky shafts of light through its smudged, partly boarded-up panes. Closer to her, on the left, stood a third door. It was shut tight, sealed up—crooked scraps of wood had been nailed haphazardly across its width from top to bottom, although Nora could still see a doorknob and hinges through the cracks. Flies buzzed thickly around it, crawled out from the thin gap left at the base of the door, where the last board didn't quite reach the floor.

The smell was intense. In high school, Nora had worked at a burger joint in summer. Her least favorite part of the job had been taking out the trash at the end of the week, when pounds upon pounds of discarded meat had been stewing in the hot dumpster for days. This smell was like that smell: so thick she could taste it, could feel it through her mouth. It left a coating on her tongue. Nora was strong-stomached, but it took a lot of effort for her not to dry-heave. For her to make herself accept the tongue-coating, the feeling, the taste, the odor.

## Corrupted Vessels

*This is the place. There's a door at the top of the stairs.*

Nora went to the boarded door and pulled on the planks. They were inexpertly though firmly attached. She cursed under her breath. The crooked way several of the nails had been hammered in would make them harder to remove.

Nora got out her phone. She retreated to the part of the hall with the tall window and began drafting her text message: it was time to get other people involved. Jamal, Nat, Mel. Friends of hers, friends of Linden's, people who had tools and wouldn't mind being woken early if it was for something important. People who would understand the urgency of the situation, wouldn't laugh at her even if she turned out to be wrong, wouldn't immediately insist on getting the cops involved. Nora's fingers clicked over the keypad, further chipping her already badly chipped nail polish.

"Put the phone *down*," hissed a voice.

Nora stifled a scream and dropped the phone, out of shock rather than compliance. She looked up, adrenaline coursing through her body, prepared to fight... and saw a child.

A kid was at the top of the stairs, stalking menacingly towards her on filthy bare feet. A white boy, maybe eleven or twelve, with a limp, straggly, overgrown mullet that reached his collarbones. He was wearing sweatpants rolled up to mid-calf and an army jacket that was too big for him, and brandishing a switchblade at her. Nora certainly wasn't going to fight a little boy. But she wasn't going to let herself get stabbed by one, either.

She held her hands up in a placating gesture and spoke calmly.

"Hey," she said. "I'm sorry I startled you. I don't mean any harm. I didn't realize anyone was here."

"You're looking for Linden," snarled the kid, making it sound like an accusation of terrible wrongdoing.

"Yes," said Nora, shocked to hear Linden's name from the kid's mouth. "Linden is my good friend. I haven't seen Linden in almost two weeks, and I'm very worried about them. Do you know Linden? Do you know where Linden is?"

The kid's free hand jerked up in a strange, tic-like motion, smoothing the breast pocket of his jacket. "No," he said, still advancing on Nora. "I don't know. Stop looking. Go away." Something in the kid's voice made Nora wonder if she'd gotten his sex wrong, if he was a girl, and older than she'd initially thought. Or was he a trans boy? She shook her head. It didn't matter. Why was she even pondering this? A kid was still a kid, and the switchblade pointed at her was still a switchblade.

"I don't want a fight," said Nora. "I'm not going to hurt you, or get you in any trouble. I only want to know what happened to my friend."

"Fuck you!"

The knife trembled in the kid's hand.

"I can leave right now," said Nora. "Just tell me what's in that room you've boarded up. Tell me where Linden is. Please."

The boy stared up at her, cheeks patchily flushed, eyes wide and crazed and so dark, the iris and pupil were hard to tell from each other.

"You know," he whispered. "You know already, don't you?" His knife wobbled less than a foot from Nora's stomach.

"I..." Nora thought fast. What response would be best? "I don't know for sure," she continued. "I only have suspicions. Like I said, I don't want to hurt you. And I don't want to get hurt. I don't want anybody to get hurt here, okay?"

The boy kept the knife where it was, and Nora noticed he was holding it much more steadily. She wasn't sure if that was a good or a bad sign.

"Make a deal," he said, voice louder now.

"What?"

"You don't want anyone to get hurt. Neither do I. So we'll make a deal. You leave here right now, and I let you go. You don't text anyone, or call anyone. You leave your phone with me, so you can't. You come back here tonight at midnight, alone, and you'll find your friend. I'll help you. You won't get hurt. And I'll give you your phone."

Nora frowned. "I'm not going to—"

The boy jabbed the knife forward. It slashed the front of Nora's shirt and left a long, shallow nick just below her breasts. Beads of blood sprouted from its ends and began to trickle down the slope of her belly.

"Ow! Jesus Christ! *Okay,* kid. Okay." The smell and the cut and the familiarity of the hall from her dream and the presence of this violent, feral child were combining to make her dizzy, nauseated, on the brink of panic. She had slipped out of reality somewhere along the line. This wasn't happening.

Nora slowly bent down, picked up her phone, and turned it off, making sure the boy could see and anticipate every movement. She set the phone on the floor again, and nudged it over to him with the toe of her boot.

"Deal," said Nora.

The boy kept the switchblade in his hand as he watched her make her way down the hall, down the stairs, out the door.

When she was in the field again, beneath the open sky, Nora started running. She ran as though she could catch the sensible, ordinary world she'd lost if she were fast enough, if her heart beat hard enough, if her sides crawled with pain. She didn't stop until she hit the pavement outside of the forest and threw up on the curb. It wasn't much. A thin, yellow-white gruel.

The sky was the color of a robin's egg. A lizard basked in the sun on top of a small concrete birdbath in someone's front yard. Stores were just opening. Children and teenagers were on their way to school. No one knew about the house in the clearing except for her, and, of course, the boy with the knife. No one really cared that Linden was missing, probably dead. The world spun on.

Nora wished she had a cigarette.

**IV.** River pulled the photograph from his pocket and made himself look it in its plastic-glossy, shadowed eyes. He tried not to think about what Linden's face might be like now. It would be worse than this washed-out mask with its lolling tongue. "Thank you," he said to the photograph. "Thanks for helping me find the gas."

The photograph didn't change or move, but he heard Linden's voice issue from it clear as anything. "No problem," they said. "Now, you have to hurry. Find Ash."

"Right." River slipped the photo back into his jacket pocket and buttoned it. He lugged the sloshing, heavy can onto the front porch. The strong smell of gasoline was a welcome relief from the rotting corpse stench of the house.

The gas had been River's idea, concocted in those desperate minutes when he'd stood down Linden's fat goth girlfriend in the upstairs hallway. But it was Linden, or Linden's ghost, or his hallucination of Linden, who had directed him to the open garage with the cans set out beside the Hummer and the convertible, the fancy worktable and the power tools, the children's bicycles and the little red wagon. Linden had told him where to look to see the cans. Linden had told him when no one was driving down the street in front of the bland stucco-and-brick mansion to which the garage belonged, when the man mowing the front lawn wasn't looking, when the boy who'd been shooting hoops in the driveway had gone inside the house for a while, when a little girl was about to come ricocheting out the front door to check the mailbox on her tiptoes. Slowly, stopping often to hide behind bushes, behind the cars, River had managed to sneak into the garage and back out with his stolen prize. He'd managed to get across town with it, through the woods to the house in the clearing, unchallenged.

Unchallenged, but not unnoticed, he thought. He wasn't an inconspicuous sight: a small, wild-looking boy muttering to himself as he walked along, clutching a big can of gasoline in his arms like it was a baby, or a pet. Although he'd switched his robe for his sweatpants and T-shirt just after they'd boarded Linden's body up in the bathroom—Ash had never mentioned the robe's abandonment, had not even seemed to notice—the clothes were still dirty, reeking. He'd been sleeping outside, or in a home that smelled of death. He hadn't had the energy to wash anything in a while, and the thought of going into town made his heart lurch more and more. He knew it was only a matter of time until someone decided he was suspicious, until someone came investigating. Until someone found them out, him and Ash, and called the cops.

Well. Someone *had* come investigating, hadn't they? So it didn't matter what the people in town thought when they saw him with the gasoline can, as long as none of them stopped him. As long as none of them came looking for him for at least a few more hours.

River looked up into the cloudless azure sky. It was probably about five p.m., he thought. Maybe six. He didn't have a watch or a phone, so he could never tell exactly what time it was without checking the clock at the public library. All the more reason to hurry. He and Ash had to get out of here well before midnight. He wished they could have gotten an even earlier start, since he didn't trust that the goth girl wouldn't go to the police.

He'd had to collect all of his and Ash's possessions before leaving for the gasoline, all that could be saved and was worth saving. He'd had to write the note and drag the little table outside. Then he'd had to find the gas and steal it.

And now he needed to find Ash, who had disappeared from their campsite at the edge of the woods that morning while he, guided by Linden's voice, had returned to the house and discovered the goth girl. He hadn't seen Ash since, though he'd checked all their usual forest hiding spots and called their name softly, over and over. He'd checked inside the house too, while he was getting their belongings out.

Nothing. No sign.

"I don't suppose you know where Ash went," he asked Linden's photograph, smoothing the fabric of its pocket with his hand. "But if you did know, you'd tell me, wouldn't you?"

Nobody answered.

River looked over at the pile of backpacks and sleeping bags, wondering again if they might not all be tainted somehow, if it might not be better to just leave them behind. Would they smell like death forever? Were there germs and worm eggs growing and thriving in the pages of his paperback novels, in the pages of his Book? He couldn't give up the Book. He couldn't give it up any more than he could the more practical supplies that he and Ash would need to survive on the road, tainted or not. And if he was taking the Book along, he might as well bring the rest of them.

River cracked his knuckles as he started back across the field. If he couldn't find Ash, it wouldn't matter what he did or didn't salvage from the house. None of it would matter. Aside from parents who would hate him if they knew who he really was and the ghost-voice of Linden's photograph, he had no one in the whole world but Ash. Ash was certainly the only one of these he wanted to be with. The only one he cared for. If Ash had left him alone here, he might as well douse his own body in the gas, flick the thumbwheel on one of his lighters, and let himself melt away.

River pulled the heads of flowers from their stalks. He walked into the woods, crushing them between his fingers, rolling them into oozing, pungent balls that stained his fingertips pinkish-purple. He assured himself that he would find Ash. He would. Soon, everything would be as it had been a couple of months earlier: back to what passed for normal. Ash would flirt with strangers, charm unsuspecting men and women with their silver hands and honeyed words, make sure that the two of them always had some cash and a place to sleep for the night. Ash would take care of everything. River just needed to get Ash out of the forest, out of this town, out of this state. Ash would feel better once they were on the road north or west, once they'd gotten away.

All River had to do was find Ash.

He let his instincts guide him. He let himself walk out past Ash's usual haunts, calling their name again every couple of minutes. Eventually, almost at the murky little creek, he thought he heard a response.

"Ash?"

The noise he'd heard came again, louder and more drawn out this time. It wasn't a word, or a voice, but a rustling, crackling sound coming from just ahead of him. If an animal was responsible for the disturbance, it would have to be a very large one. River looked wildly around, squinted and then opened his eyes until they watered from the strain of it, but he saw nothing. Only trees and dirt, more trees and dirt. A squirrel running across the ground.

"Ash?"

A rush of displaced air. A choked, gargling sob of a sound. A snap. A body tumbled from the branches of an oak, rope noosed around its neck. Thick banner of copper hair, striking even when unwashed for weeks and beginning to grow together in mats. Arms and legs skinny and white as if they were already just bones.

"Ash!" River's heart caught in his throat as he ran forward, tripped, stumbled, came to rest kneeling on the ground beside Ash, who lay like a dropped marionette, moaning softly and clutching at pebbles, at twigs, at soil. They were alive. River saw in an instant that the snapping he'd heard had been the branch Ash had chosen to tie their rope around, and not Ash's neck, giving way.

The broken branch had not landed on top of Ash. That was a very good thing. Even though it hadn't been able to hold Ash's full, unsupported weight, it looked more than thick and heavy enough to do some real damage if it hit a person. River took a second to glare at the branch where it lay splintered and scabby-barked in the dirt. He hated the branch, and he wished it ill. It had almost killed his beloved.

Ash was crying. They murmured incoherently through their tears and made no movement to rise. Snot bubbled from their nose. River reached out tenderly to wipe it away.

"Ash? Hey, Ash, talk to me. What are you doing? Are you hurt? Can you sit up?"

Ash nodded. They sat up slowly, not looking at River. "I'm sorry," they muttered. "I truly am, River. I don't want to leave you like this. You're only a child."

"Then *don't! Don't leave me!* I was just coming to find you! We're going to get out of here tonight! I have a plan, Ash! We're going to put this whole situation with Linden behind us. And I'm not a child." He took Ash's hand in both of his. They let him. "This isn't like you, Ash. You've always told me suicide is for the spiritually unenlightened."

Ash made a hoarse barking sound that took River a moment to recognize as a laugh. He had never heard Ash laugh that way before.

"I am the spiritually unenlightened." Tears continuing to roll from their red-rimmed, bloodshot blue eyes. "The angels left me. They're *gone*, River. I haven't heard them since... since we... since *I* killed Linden. Since I burned Linden's clothes. At first I thought it was because I had fucked up. Linden was supposed to come live with us, and then we were all three supposed to find the vessel of air together. I failed, so the angels abandoned us all, to create a new set of vessels, to try again." Ash shuddered and leaned into River's shoulder. River put his arms around Ash and held on tight. They had never felt so small and frail to him before. He had never been the comforter instead of the comforted.

"Then," Ash's muffled whisper rose to his ear, "*then* I started to think something worse. River, I started to think maybe I had made this whole thing up inside my head. Maybe there's something *wrong* with me. Maybe

I had started pretending one day and I had pretended for so long that I forgot it wasn't real, that I had started to see and hear the angels, I..." They laughed in that strange, hoarse way again. "I killed Linden for nothing, and now they're dead for no reason, to no purpose. I've never done *anything* for a purpose. There were never any angels. I'm not special. I'm a murderer."

"No!" said River, too sharply. Then, his hands in Ash's hair, speaking in his most soothing voice, "Ash, no. You are special. I believe in you. I believe we've been chosen for something remarkable."

"Why? You don't know anything, River. Why have faith in me?"

"Because I *do* know something. Ash, I hear voices, too." Well, *a* voice.

"The angels," said Ash, voice a mix of naked skepticism and cautious hope. They moved away from him a little, stared at him with a watery, exhausted, but still piercing gaze. River saw the green and brown of foliage behind them, the growing shadows. He heard nothing but Ash's breathing and the faint trickle of the little creek. He made himself steady for what he knew he had to do.

"Yeah," he said. "Ash, I hear the angels now. I see them, too. They're writhing in the trees and the telephone wires. They're lying slick as fish in puddles, all their lidless eyes looking back at me." He thought of what Ash had told him in the past, all the things Ash had said half-tranced on a stranger's couch or crouched in the corner of a Walmart parking lot, scrawling symbols on the ground with a nub of chalk. "I even smell the angels, Ash. I taste them."

"What do they taste like, River?"

"Black licorice," he answered, reaching out to touch Ash's tear-soaked cheek. "Black licorice and honey."

Ash nodded, and leaned against the palm of River's hand. He thought he saw the beginning of a smile twitch at the corners of their lips.

"That's right," they said.

"They tell me things, Ash. They told me you made a mistake with Linden, but it's all right. Linden will go back to the earth. Their spirit will be happier there. We tried our best. Sometimes even prophets fuck up." River took a deep breath. "That's no reason to commit suicide, Ash. We can fix this. The angels told me what to do. If we hurry, we can get out of here tonight. Come on. Stand up."

Slow and jerky on their feet, Ash obeyed. River's stomach and heart twinged when he saw just how much they'd degraded since Linden's death. They were cadaverous themself, their red robe so ragged it was almost indecent, with huge storm-cloud bags beneath their eyes and faint lines on their forehead River was sure had never been there before. Even the rings on their fingers had become badly tarnished.

River's own legs felt strong and sturdy beneath him. He was wearing his shoes, but that almost didn't matter. The soles of his feet were like leather. His palms were small but callused. He could have sworn he'd even grown taller recently, though he thought that was probably wishful thinking.

River took Ash's hand and began to lead them home—or back to the house, at least. It wasn't their home anymore. Soon, it wouldn't be anything.

As they walked, River told Ash what they were going to do next. Both Ash and Linden's voices stayed silent.

"I should be the one to do this part," Ash said, with a touch of their old authority. It was sunset now. Ash and River stood together on the front porch of the house, both breathing open-mouthed. River had just picked up the gas can and opened the front door. He looked at Ash, a little surprised.

"Why?"

"Fire is my element. This is my right," Ash told him, or maybe they said "rite."

"Uh…" River could follow his friend's reasoning, but he recalled the noose, the snapping tree branch. He remembered his own thoughts of pouring the gasoline over his body and setting it alight. He didn't think he trusted Ash with the can.

"Smart boy," said Linden from his pocket. River did his best not to react to the sudden return of their commentary.

"Didn't the angels tell you? I would think the angels would have told you to hand the fire over to me."

River thought quickly.

"Yes," he said. "You get to pour the gas and strike the flame. But I have to come with you through the house. I have to stay beside you the whole time, and the lighter has to stay in my pocket until the very end. We'll use the green one. Green for water, green for leaves."

Ash nodded.

"So it shall be done."

They held out their arms to take the can. River handed it over, reluctantly. The sky was bloody, feverish, already aflame.

"You two had better get this started real fuckin' fast," said Linden. "You're almost out of luck. Nora's decided not to keep her promise after all."

*You don't know that,* thought River. *You can't know that. Shut up.*

"We have to hurry," he told Ash, as they stepped inside the house for the last time.

Through the living room, Ash splashing ribbons of gasoline over the armchair, startling roaches and spiders. Flies buzzed cautiously around the ceiling's perimeter in thick swarms, curious about the warm-skinned intruders but avoiding the petrol. The twin candles in their bottle-holders fell over when River stumbled near them—Ash stomped on the downed bottles with their boots until the glass fragmented, not gleeful, not angry, but with a businesslike determination. River thought of the teacups in the yard, now mostly obscured by mud and rapidly growing spring weeds. Through the foyer now, retracing their steps. Through the kitchen, gasoline dousing dry brown sink-plants, floorboards, cabinets and their contents.

"Lucky so much of this place is wood," Linden observed. "Lucky the roof doesn't leak much at all. It should burn all right."

*Shut up. I'm going to leave you as soon as we're done here. Maybe throw your stupid dead face in the flames.*

"I don't think you will," said Linden. "I don't think you'll do that at all. I think you've come to depend on me."

"Ash," River said, his voice too loud, "be sure to save a little of the gas for upstairs.

"I will." Ash had already moved on to the room of the Auspicious Window.

The can made sloshing sounds as Ash made methodical spiral shapes on the floor and over the diminished altar. The flowers had all withered or rotted and the water in its cup was two-thirds evaporated. Apart from those things, the offerings remained where they'd been placed. The Window still rainbowed them with ethereal glitter, especially psychedelic at the sunset's peak. Nonetheless, the altar seemed to have lost some fundamental quality it had once had. River struggled to remember what it had looked like when it had felt impressive, holy, numinous. Surely it hadn't been such a sad, clumsy assemblage of trash before. It didn't even look like art—it looked like a crude play structure contrived by a disturbed and not very capable child.

The Window above it had lost none of its majesty, which made River resent the Window, looming there all proud and grand. Making Ash's creation look more pitiful by contrast. Earlier, he had thought wistfully of how it would be nice if they could somehow save the Window, or at least a part of it, some jagged piece of pane to take with them on their travels. Now, he hoped the fire ruined it, melted all the candied glass into blackened goop or exploded it like a bomb.

"It's too bad about the Window," Ash said, and sighed.

River scowled. "Let's do the top story quick, okay?"

Upstairs, the flies were clotted around the boarded up door, and the smell was so bad River felt faint. It coated his tongue like a flavor. Ash looked queasy too, but extended a long hand to brush the crooked two-by-fours, the heads of bent nails. "We still have that claw hammer," they said softly. "River, should we... should we open it?" They looked down at him with wide, trusting eyes, and River realized that no matter what he said now, yes or no, Ash would go along without any resistance.

He hesitated. Part of him was curious to see what Linden's corpse looked like now. He tried to imagine, and failed. Ribcage and stomach caved in, filled with maggots and decaying organic soup? Leathery mummy skin stretched tight over bones? Bloated and mottled, features expanded beyond recognition, flies creeping out from between hugely swollen lips, eyelids, labia? A skeleton with some scraps of flesh hanging from it like the tatters of Ash's robe? Strangely, horribly, he realized he wanted to see.

"No," said Linden. "Over my dead body. Pun intended. Leave it be."

"No," River found himself saying to Ash. "No, we keep it shut. Whatever's in there will still burn."

River thought he saw a faint glimmer of relief in Ash's gaze. They nodded, and turned to enter the bedroom. The last of the gas flowed over mattress and loose paper, a few stray items of Ash's clothing that River hadn't packed, the corpses of flies and other insects mounded on the floor in dark little drifts. Ash shook the can upside-down as they walked backwards out of the bedroom, backwards down the hallway, past the boarded bathroom door again. Finally, there wasn't a drop of gasoline left. Ash let the can fall. It made a series of hollow thuds as it tumbled down the stairs. The light was growing dimmer by the second. River was dizzy, balloon-headed, suddenly claustrophobic.

"Good," said Linden. "You need to leave *now*."

"Come on." River took Ash's hand and pulled them downstairs, through the door, onto the front porch. Dozens of roaches scurried out alongside them in a mass exodus. Roaches, River reflected, were smart. They knew when to get out of places. That was part of why they were so hard to kill.

Ash and River stood facing the house. It looked like a huge, nauseating wedding cake, River thought, collapsing slowly into the earth.

"May I have the lighter now?" asked Ash.

River handed them the dark green Bic. Ash thumbed the wheel expertly. It hissed and sparked, flared. Ash knelt and lit the edge of a gasoline trail. The fire whooshed up and onward. Ash stood, and River pulled them backwards off the porch, into the safe, shadowed grass.

The two friends watched for a moment. Licks of flame had already begun to appear through the house's front windows. A shimmer of heat distorted the gingerbread trim, the rusty doorknob, the peeling paint. The fire reflected in Ash's eyes, turning them violet. Ash's mouth hung open in awe.

"You did that," said River, hugging Ash to him. "See? You are a powerful being."

Ash nodded, but River wasn't sure if they'd really heard.

"Hey," he said, tugging Ash's arm gently, "I put our bags over by the tree line there—the side of the field towards the highway. There are a few shirts and some pants in your bag. Go change. The robe'll attract too much attention."

Ash stood swaying, humming.

"Come on," River said, with a sharper tug. "The angels say you have to."

"All right," Ash said and shook him off. They wandered away to the backpacks, and River hoped it wasn't wishful thinking that made him see their step as lighter than it had been before they'd torched the house, their back held straighter.

"Now," River whispered, addressing the photograph in his pocket, "It's time to take care of you."

The small table sat in a splotch of mostly plant-free dirt near the edge of the clearing closest to the trail into town. Squinting in the grainy twilight, River removed the note he'd written from one of his side pockets and unfolded it:

DEAR NORA,

YOUR FRIEND LINDEN IS DEAD. I KNOW YOUR NAME BECAUSE THEY TOLD ME. I'M SORRY FOR YOUR LOSS. DON'T COME LOOKING FOR ME, OR FOR ANYONE ELSE.

SINCERELY,

JACK

## Corrupted Vessels

River couldn't sign the note with a name he still used, but it would have felt wrong not to sign it at all. He took the photograph from his breast pocket and slipped it beneath the letter, then put them both on top of the table. He weighed them down with Nora's phone. She'd find it, he was certain. How she reacted was none of his concern. He and Ash would be far away by then. Maybe even across the state line.

"Wait," called Linden's voice as River turned to walk across the field. "Where are you going? You're not going to leave me here, are you? I told you, you can't get rid of me."

River ignored Linden's voice. He started to sing to himself under his breath.

Linden's cries grew no fainter as he approached Ash, but, sometime on Ash and River's journey through the woods to the highway, they did eventually stop. River's heart could have flown from his chest when he realized. It could have burst into joyous confetti. Even tripping over roots, stepping in mud past his ankles, seeing the eerie gleam of carnivorous eyes in the dark—even these things inspired giddy relief. It was all going to work out. Everything was really going to be okay.

"Look," said Ash, stopping and turning. "Just for a second, River. Look at that." They pointed behind them, through the snarl of black branches. The dim glow of firelight shimmered in the distance. River thought he could even see smoke and flame rising up past the tops of the trees. A scent of burning was heavy in the air, and somewhere, related or not, a siren wailed.

"Yeah," said River. "It's kind of beautiful, isn't it?"

"Do you see the angels in the fire? In the smoke?"

"Of course I do, Ash. Of course. Let's hurry."

They held hands and journeyed on.

Reddish pink light of dawn, sunset's opposite, and River hadn't slept between the one and the other, though Ash lay curled and softly snoring in the back seat of the trucker's cab. River sat up front, next to the trucker himself, watching the sky burn and bleed into a brand new day through the rearview mirror. Sparkles and smushed bugs lined the edge of the windshield, framing the long black road and the broad crop and cattle fields on either side, the brightening air.

"You and your big sister heading out west for any particular reason, son?" the trucker asked. He was a weathered middle-aged man, skinny, with a couple days' worth of beard stubble and Coke-bottle glasses. "You don't have to answer if you don't want. I'm just curious. That one back there, now, she does look like the California type."

"We've got family in California," said River, the lie springing easily to his tongue. "Texas, too. Aunts and uncles. Our parents are dead."

"Oh," said the trucker, without any discernible change in emotional affect. "Well, that is truly a pity. I am sorry to hear about that."

"It's okay," said River. "It happened a long time ago."

His scalp itched, and he scratched hard at it. No, maybe it wasn't his scalp after all. Maybe the itch was somewhere deeper, down beneath the bone of his skull. He squirmed in the passenger seat.

The trucker said something he didn't quite catch.

"Pardon?" River asked.

"I didn't say nothing."

"And it's well I sing, bonny boys, bonny mad boys," sang the voice, which didn't belong to the trucker after all. "Bedlam boys are bonny! For they all go bare, and they live by the air, and they want no drink nor money!"

Linden had never been inside the photograph, attached to the photograph. Of course not. It had been silly of him to think so. He smacked himself in the side of the head. "Shut up," he growled, under his breath.

The trucker shot him a quick, concerned glance. "You need a nap, son? You can switch with your sister at this next stop, get a couple hours of sleep before I have to leave you two and get on my way. You've been awake since the middle of the night."

River had been awake for longer. He didn't feel as though he could ever sleep again, would ever want to sleep again. Still, he found his head nodding up and down, his mouth opening. "Yeah," his mouth said. "Yeah, I think I'd like that."

"I'll see you in your dreams," said Linden's voice. River ignored it, gritting his teeth. In the rearview mirror, he saw Ash's eyelids flutter, their lips begin to work. "Linden?" murmured Ash, soft and sleep-fuzzy. "Linden, are you there?"

"No," said River. "It's me. It's only me."

"River." Ash half sat, blinking rapidly. "Little River. You're here."

"That's right," he said, through Linden's resumed singing, through the sudden fatigue that fell upon him like a smothering cloud. The road carried them away.

Thick, oily black smoke was rising from somewhere

just beyond the horizon, but this fire had nothing to do with them. There were all kinds of fires, for all kinds of reasons, everywhere.

"I'm with you, Ash," said River.

# New Eden

You wouldn't think it was a wasteland out beyond the gate and the wall. That's what Zillah says, and it's hard to disagree. In here, everything's green and fine. Mostly even when the weather gets weird. One summer, a sudden snow killed a bunch of the crops. It'd all melted away a week later, and a week after that, you wouldn't have known anything was different in the forest just by looking. Only the fields seemed ruined.

That was a long time ago. Most of us were real little. Zillah and Patience were eight and nine, so they remember it best. Patience especially—her half-brother died when we were all so hungry later, and then the only boy child left was Adam. But things are blooming now, and the corn is growing higher. The weird weather hasn't hurt us in a while.

The sky is the color of Adam's eyes, which all us girls love to look at. Except for Patience, who says she's too old for him, and Zillah, who says she won't ever go mushy over a man.

Zillah says a lot of things. She says she saw three deer today while she was making her rounds—two does and a fawn. And she saw rabbits, woodchucks, songbirds. She even saw a fox with her kits, Zillah says. All this inside the compound. Zillah saw several frogs by the creek, most of which had a normal number of legs and no tumors. The wall can't make that much difference, says Zillah. The world must be coming back on the other side, too.

Dorcas listens to her sister—they're full sisters, not half—with her mouth stuck in a skeptical twist. Dorcas is much prettier than Zillah. Taller and more filled out, even though she's four years younger. She tries to be pious, and if not pious, then practical. We think if Adam loves any of us back, she's the one. But Dorcas was betrothed to Father Joshua this year, and their wedding is to follow her fifteenth birthday in October. Dorcas is honored to be chosen as Father Joshua's fourth wife. She says so all the time.

Dorcas would never make a move on Adam now. That would be as good as adultery. Dorcas hardly even looks at Adam anymore. But Adam tries to needle Dorcas sometimes—make her admit she remembers him. Now he's telling Zillah he thinks she could be right, slinging an arm around Zillah's broad waist, asking if she's ever thought about trying to go through the gate, or over the wall.

"Sure." Zillah stares at him with her small, dark eyes. It is not a soft or romantic stare. "All the time, recently. The only question is how. I doubt I can get Father Joshua to open the gate for me. I've been looking for cracks or gaps in the wall. Or places where the surface is rough enough to be climbable. I've been practicing my climbing."

"Stop telling lies," says Dorcas. "Do you want to go to Hell?"

"I don't lie," says Zillah. "I don't lie, and I'm not sure there is a Hell at all."

Dorcas makes an affronted noise that doesn't fool anybody. She cannot bring herself to be surprised, or even scandalized. She knows her sister too well.

"So," Zillah continues, leaning uncomfortably close to Adam's face. "Why are you asking? Do you want to come with me? I bet you're a better climber than I am."

"I have to help work the fields." Adam scoots away

quick, back to the edge of the old picnic table bench. Little Hallie moves from where she's been sitting cross-legged on top of the table, and gets between them, glares at Zillah. "You *will* go to Hell," she says.

"You're eleven." Zillah laughs. "What do you know?" She ruffles Hallie's cornsilk hair, heedless of her sour pouting.

When the gong rings out from the main hall, our rest break is over. We get up and go back to work.

It's kind of strange that Zillah and Patience still hang out with the rest of us kids. By the standards of the dead world, they'd be grown women. By the standards of the compound, they're both more than old enough to marry. But they're still girls, and maybe they'll always be girls. Father Joshua won't betroth Patience because of her crazy, crippled mother. And nobody wants Zillah, who's unbelievably ugly and probably barren besides. She's never had Eve's curse. Once she pointed this out to Father Joshua when he was rebuking her for some transgression, maybe wearing Adam's spare pair of jeans or trying to ride one of the two plow horses. He was on her about rebellion and sinfulness. She asked if she wasn't the most free of sin in the community, since God had seen fit to spare her from the problems of manhood *and* from monthly bleeding. "I'm a clean slate," she said. "That's better than even you can claim."

For that, Father Joshua had Brother Ethan and Brother Paul beat her in front of the main hall until her will was broken, along with some small bones in her left hand. Zillah apologized and said the penitent prayers.

But she didn't mean them, and she was back to her old self by the time her hand had healed into a crooked but workable claw.

Maybe that's another reason she sticks with us, instead of befriending the married women. They're too grown up to rebel or have wills that need breaking. They know their place in the community. Besides, they're usually with their husbands or co-wives.

Sometimes, lately, when Patience gets a short break from taking care of her mother and Zillah is done with her trapping and foraging and patrolling and household chores for the day, the two of them go off alone together. Hallie and Sharon have seen them following the river deep into the woods. Maybe they even go out as far as the wall.

Patience is easygoing and almost pretty, if you ignore the lazy eye and the bad teeth. She never makes trouble. We all hope she'll be a good influence on Zillah, that Zillah won't persuade her to do anything dangerous or stupid.

At nightfall, after all the day's work is done, we gather around a bonfire and listen to Father Joshua sermonize. He's the only one of the men without a beard. With his round face and bald scalp, it makes him look almost babyish, but he's tall and his eyes are piercing, changeable in color as the river water. He has all these tattoos on his hands and arms that he incorporates into the sermons. Snakes and apples. The words love and hate. Christ on the cross. Something with long talons and four wings covering its face.

His voice dips up and down with the flames as he tells the community again how we alone in all the world have been spared from Hell. We're in a period of tribulation, waiting for God to lift us up into the air with Him. The land across the wall belongs to Satan and death: it's ruin, it's illusion. We children are blessed in our innocence, but the adults remember. Some of the men at the back of the crowd nod gravely. The men stand the farthest from Father Joshua and the fire, then the women, then us kids, girls and boy. That's in order of how much we need Father Joshua's guidance and protection, he says.

Adam keeps sneaking glances at Dorcas, and we think he looks very beautiful in the flickering light. We think he looks like Father Joshua's tattooed Christ, but without the blood and agony, and only the faint beginnings of reddish stubble on his chin.

Dorcas glances back at him once. She makes a face none of us know how to read: an adult kind of face, or even a Zillah kind of face. After that, she keeps her gaze trained on Father Joshua. She looks focused, rapt. She looks like she is trying to make herself love him the way we love Adam. It should be easy: he's the one with the word of God in his mouth. But he also has the head of a giant baby. He has three wives already, sitting in a silent row behind him, wearing identical pastel dresses: green, yellow, pink. We suspect Dorcas's will be pale blue. Sometimes it seems like maybe Father Joshua is just collecting the prettiest women for himself, like maybe he doesn't care about them as individual people all that much. Well, maybe that's what God wants. But it must make it harder for Dorcas.

"I'm glad I'm not pretty," Sharon whispers to Hallie. "Or ugly. I'm glad I'm just in the middle." Hallie nods, and Sarah shushes them both. We all agree with her though. We all know what she's thinking, what she means.

Father Joshua doesn't have any kids, even though he has the most wives. We think maybe he's putting his hopes on Dorcas for that. It's weird to imagine either of them with a baby.

Sometimes, we wonder if Father Joshua's wives have ever had demons come out of them. Most of the other women have, several more than once. Demons seem like regular pregnancies until they're born, and then you find out Satan played a trick. Instead of a baby, you get something like the mutant frogs. Too many limbs or not enough, or a too-small head, or a tail, or purple splotches all over its skin and a big twisted gash through its upper lip. One of the Brothers, or Father Joshua himself, comes and takes the demon away. To put it back in Hell, we think. Or maybe to put it on the other side of the wall, which amounts to much the same thing.

Summer moves on and we all get hot and sweaty and irritable. Adam takes his shirt off in the fields and we aren't supposed to look at his back and his arms moving, the heave of his brown, freckly stomach. But we do. We hide in the blackberry bushes and watch when we can get away with it.

We talk to Dorcas about her wedding, how excited

she is, what flowers she wants to carry, what *exactly* it is a man and a woman do the night after they get married. Dorcas doesn't want to tell us, or maybe she doesn't know yet.

Hallie finds some long, black reptile in the tall grass after a rain, and we argue about whether it's a snake (bad, like the serpent who tempted Eve) or a lizard (okay, we don't think there are any important lizards in the Bible). It looks like a snake but it has stubby little legs that don't work well. We decide it's a lizard and keep it as a secret pet until it dies.

We mostly forget about Zillah and her idea of crossing the wall. We don't see her as much, and she doesn't talk about it when we do. She's started helping Patience with her shaking, ranting mother. And Patience helps Zillah keep watch, forage the forest, set and check her traps. They are their own little group of two.

One day in the middle of August, Zillah and Patience come out of the woods together and approach the picnic table, where we are gathered, as we often are, on our break. There's a third person slung between them, his left arm over Patience's shoulders and his right arm over Zillah's. His feet limp along in the dirt. One of his ankles is twisted around wrong. A little white nodule of bone shows bright through a bloody tear in his skin.

We know right away he's not one of the community's men. His clothes are dirty but still too new-looking. He's got a chin blue with stubble but no beard. We stare dumbfounded until the three-headed beast of them's almost at the table and we can see milky sweat blobs on the man's forehead. Wormy red veins in his grayish green eyes. He smells bad. He has teeth so white we think they might be fake.

"Who's he?" hisses Dorcas. "Zillah!" Her whole body trembles.

"The devil," whispers Sarah. "The devil has found us. We need to tell Father Joshua."

"Like Hell we do," says Zillah. "He said his name is Eddie. He's from a city outside the compound."

"He broke his ankle climbing over the wall," adds Patience. "Move over, Hallie, Sarah, Mary. He needs to sit."

"There aren't actually cities anymore, are there?" asks Mary.

"He climbed the wall?" asks Sharon.

"Can't he talk for himself?" asks Hallie.

"How can you be sure he's not the devil?" asks Sarah.

The man's eyelashes flutter and his bloodshot eyes roll up beneath them. He moans, low and animal-like.

"Please," he chokes out through his white, white teeth.

"Move!" snaps Patience. We're so surprised that we do. None of us have ever heard Patience raise her voice before. She and Zillah arrange Eddie so he's sitting in the clear space on the bench. He sighs and groans.

"I'm going back home to get some of Mama's tonic," says Patience. "Bandages, too. You all stay here."

Zillah nods. Patience runs off, holding her muddy skirt immodestly above her knees. The picnic table is under an oak in the low valley at the edge of the woods. Once she's over the rise of the grassy hill, on her way to the fields and the buildings beyond them, we can't see her anymore.

"It's incredible that you're here," gasps Eddie. "Incredible. Old backwoods cult commune. Must've been sealed up for twenty, twenty-five years."

"We're supposed to be the only people left on Earth," says Hallie. "You have some explaining to do."

"Don't make him talk yet!" says Dorcas, her compassion overcoming her fear. Or maybe it's loyalty to her sister overcoming her fear. Zillah's at the treeline, picking up big fallen branches and stacking them in a pile. She won't want to miss what Eddie has to say. "He's in a lot of pain."

"He'll talk later," says Adam, trying to sound manly and authoritative. "He'll tell us everything, or we will get Father Joshua and have him cast out into the wasteland again."

"Incredible," says Eddie again. A hoarse laugh squeezes itself out of his mouth behind the word. He tilts his head back and closes his eyes, and then he doesn't say anything else for a long time, not even when Hallie pokes inside his ears.

He doesn't say anything until after Patience has liberally spooned tonic into his mouth and salved and splinted his ankle. Until after it becomes clear what Zillah's doing at the edge of the woods: she's building a little sleeping shelter, disguised with pine needles and an artful arrangement of rocks and loose sticks near the entrance. It's the kind of shelter Zillah builds for herself sometimes, when she wants to spend the night in the forest. She's not supposed to, but she's sneaky about it and beatings can't stop her.

"It's for you," Zillah explains to Eddie, who is taking deep breaths through his nose and staring at his ankle, then at her, then at Patience. "You can't go into the central settlement with us. It's not safe."

"No," says Eddie. "You don't understand, Miss..."

"Zillah. Don't worry, Patience and I will bring you food when we can, until you're healed up some."

"And I thank you for your kindness," says Eddie, forcefully. His accent is strange. "But let me why I've come here. Please."

My full name's Edward Tinsley Jr., as in the Tinsley Fairweather—well, that'd mean something to you if you hadn't grown up in here. It'd mean something to your parents, probably. My father made his fortune on these patented lightweight, portable, solar-powered air conditioning units. So I've never had to work, lived twenty-three years in a paradise dome outside... the name of the city doesn't matter any more than Tinsley, I suppose. You won't know it. But even as a kid, I wanted something bigger, some purpose in my life, some danger.

I remember being seven or eight, during one of those crisis periods, watching huge storms coming west from the coast through the safe, curved wall of the dome. It was bright inside, with a gentle breeze and a small meadow of nodding flowers all around me. But outside there were black clouds piled into spires as tall as the skyscrapers I'd seen in the city the one time Dad took me there with him. They looked like they were boiling, on the edge of changing shape into dragons or giants. The brightness was safe, and it was false, and it bored me. I wanted to go out beneath the massing dragons in the sky.

Once I got older, finished school, moved into my own apartment, there was nothing stopping me. I'd done the usual dome teen partying, gone on a few tame joyrides outside. But that wasn't what I really wanted. I practiced my parkour and my climbing, learned to tell when a stair was solid or rotten, learned to walk real quiet, heel-toe. I bought some equipment. I started doing urban exploration with a couple of guys who were looking for treasure in the run-down remains of the suburbs. I wasn't looking for treasure, at least not in the same sense. I wanted to see the remains of the real, old way of life, before climate control and comfort and happypills. I wish we hadn't ruined it all.

I used to sit in old churches and look up at the big, intricate colored-glass windows. Used to imagine animals like horses and dogs, and men who worked with their hands. Almost wished I'd been born poor—I mean, I know how fucked up that is, but if I'd been born outside the dome I'd've grown up around all the beautiful old things.

So one day the guys told me about this place. It's kind of a ghost story for them, y'see—two days' journey, and they don't bother going that far from the city. Besides, you were supposed to be this ascetic sect, not much in the way of valuable property to speak of.

They said your leaders bought a bunch of forested land out in the middle of nowhere thirty years ago, started building a wall around it a few years later. Eventually stopped coming out around the time of the last plague. Nobody knew what happened, if the plague had gotten every last soul inside the compound, or if you were still here. Living separately, like dome people. But honestly, like people from the time before. Traditional values, no modern technology. Belief in higher powers, respect for nature.

I hoped it was the second one, but I expected I'd find a tomb. The guys agreed. Still, it'd been long enough that all the plague germs would be dead, and maybe I would discover things of value to me.

I made the trek. I found the wall. It was craggy, covered in thick vines that would be easy to climb. I camped out at its base and went over the next morning. Wasn't expecting the sheer drop on this side. The stone's been sanded and polished, or something. I fell. I found you.

*I found you.*

You're so beautiful, you have no idea. I've never seen girls— young women—like you before. Never in my life. You're so pure.

Please. I know you're suspicious of outsiders, but I mean you no harm. I want to join you, if you'll have me. I'm fit, and I'm strong, and I'm quick. I know I'm capable of working the land. I believe in God, or at least I believe I can learn to believe. Take me to your leader. Let me petition him. I know he'll have mercy and let me stay. All I've ever wanted is a simple, natural life, devoted to something larger than myself.

We're all kind of shocked into silence once Eddie's through talking. Dorcas and Zillah are both frowning: the same family frown on a pretty face and an ugly one. Adam's nervously picking at the beds of his fingernails. It's Sarah who finally speaks.

"Lies," she says. "You're lying. Testing us."

"I promise you I'm not," says Eddie.

Patience spoons more medicine between Eddie's cracked lips. He shivers.

"We can't take you to Father Joshua," says Zillah. "We can't. You don't know what you're asking. He would kill you."

"Maybe not!" says Hallie. She pets Eddie's hair. "I believe you, Mr. Eddie. Father Joshua is merciful, like Jesus. If he knows you're not a demon, I bet he'll let you stay."

Zillah scowls at the tangled grass around Eddie's lamed foot.

"Eddie," says Dorcas, gently. "Mr. Fairweather." She stands and walks around the picnic table so that she's in front of him, her wavy chestnut hair blowing around her neck where it's escaped from its braid. She gives him her best smile and sticks her chest out a little. "Your arrival comes as a surprise to all of us. It would be better if you waited here for a day or so while we figure out what to do. Perhaps you'll be allowed to stay, since we have so few men below fifty. But you must wait."

Adam shoots up and hurries clumsily to her side. "That's right," he says, pitching his voice lower than usual. "We can't rush this. You're an invalid. We have no way of knowing whether your story is true."

"It's obviously true," says Zillah irritably. "In its outline, if not in every specific." She addresses Eddie again. "The important thing is, you don't want to live here. You have no idea what it's really like. You wouldn't be happy..." Zillah trails off. She swallows and starts again. "It's more of a trap than your dome. You can't come and go as you please."

Patience puts her hand on Zillah's shoulder. To our mild surprise, Zillah leans into it. She even rests her head on Patience's chest, as though she's much younger than she is and very tired.

"Sour grapes," mutters Eddie. None of us know what that means. "Probably can't find a husband." Then, louder: "Beautiful girl, what's your name?" He gestures at Dorcas.

"Dorcas," says Dorcas. "Dorcas Harlow. Soon to be Dorcas Pentecost."

"Congratulations." The word goes soft and slurry in the middle. "He's a lucky man, that Mr. Pentecost."

"Father Joshua," says Dorcas. "Father."

Eddie doesn't seem to hear. His eyelids are drooping. Patience's mother's tonic is powerful stuff.

Patience and Zillah lift Eddie under his arms and walk him over to the little shelter Zillah built. They help him lie down inside. They put him on his back, so we can still see his beautiful face through a thatch of branches. The lump in his throat is bobbing up and down like a piece of unchewed food that got stuck in there. It's called an Adam's apple, that lump, even though Adam doesn't really have one. Maybe the real Adam did, the first one, at the beginning of the world.

"Eddie's apple," says Sharon.

We all giggle nervously.

"If he stays, I want to marry him," says Hallie. "Not for a few years, though. When I'm Dorcas's age."

"You don't get to decide who you marry," says Mary.

"Well, I'll ask Father Joshua, of course."

"Father Joshua doesn't decide either. God does."

Hallie sighs. "Right."

Zillah clears her throat to get our attention. Then she makes us all put our hands over our hearts and swear not to tell anyone about Eddie. We're not sure if we're going to keep this promise or not. Maybe Eddie is a demon. Besides, it feels wrong to keep secrets from Father Joshua and the Brothers. But doesn't God speak to them? Won't God tell them all about Eddie if they really need to know? We like having Eddie here. We like looking at him. Maybe he'll tell us more stories when he wakes up.

Most of us have never had a real secret before. It feels exciting. Wrong and exciting. We have trouble sleeping after lights out. We turn over and over on our beds in the dark, listening to owls and crickets. We wonder if Eddie is listening to them, too.

When afternoon comes around again, we go back to visit him. Eddie's doing bad. The bandage around his ankle has dried blood and pus on it. The pus is shiny and the blood is like flaking rust. He drinks the water we've brought him, but doesn't touch the bread. His face looks grayish and rumpled, and he won't talk to any of us except Dorcas, who he begs for tonic. Dorcas tries to explain that it's Patience who has the tonic, not her, but he doesn't seem to understand. Even after Patience finally spoons it into his mouth, it's Dorcas he's looking at. "Thank you," he keeps saying. "My little savior. Thank you."

Dorcas blushes. "I didn't do anything," she says to a space in the branches a few feet above Eddie's head.

Hallie nudges Sarah in the ribs. "He's not a demon,"

she says. "You can see he's really hurt and sick. He's too pitiful to not be human."

"He could be pretending," Sarah says.

"I can hear everything you girls are saying," says Eddie.

Hallie gets down on her haunches right next to him. She notices his eyes are the same color as the lichen that grows on parts of the wall. His breath is like a dead frog rotting in the heat.

"We'll get you some teeth cleaning paste later," she says.

"Just bring me into your settlement, please," says Eddie. "I know this seems like a game, but I need to talk to your leader. Man to man." He shoots a glance at Zillah. "He won't kill me if he hears me out."

"Do you have anything from the world outside the wall?" asks Hallie.

"What?"

"Like a map or a letter from out there to prove you're a real person from a real city, not a demon. Something to show us, and to show Father Joshua."

"A demon could create a map or a letter," says Sarah.

Everyone ignores her.

Eddie smiles with all his fake-looking teeth. "I have something much better," he says. He's sitting up, wincing, rummaging around in the many pockets that march down his pant legs. "Aha!" He takes out a little thing made of metal and plastic. It's disc-shaped. It has rubber buttons on the side, a smooth dark circle in the center. None of us know what it is. A toy?

Eddie presses one of the buttons, and the little thing makes a noise like a bird. Skinny rays of light shoot out of the circle, and Hallie, who was leaning right over it, leaps back with a shout. The rays of light make a picture in the air. More than a picture: there's a little castle or fortress or something in front of us suddenly, a collection of tall, glittering towers. Hallie immediately tries to touch them, but her hand just falls through.

"There's nothing *there*," she says in wonder. Sarah and Mary are holding hands, trembling, their eyes wide.

"It's a hologram," says Eddie. "Just a photo, but if I open the cache, I can—"

"We don't know what any of that means," Zillah interrupts. "Tell me what I'm looking at."

"Part of downtown," says Eddie. "Some of the nicer buildings." He presses another button and the image turns so we're seeing it from a new angle. There are tiny people in the tiny windows of the towers.

Sarah and Mary are backing away, retreating to the safety of the picnic table.

Zillah and Patience exchange a look.

"You can't show this to Father Joshua," Zillah says. "Listen, wait one more day, all right? I promise we'll figure something out."

Eddie is about to complain, but Patience promises him a supply of extra tonic for overnight and he calms down quick. *Tomorrow,* we all think. *Tomorrow we'll find out what's going to happen to him.*

What happens is that Eddie disappears.

We run to see him during the break, racing each other through the long grass and the wild Queen Anne's Lace. When we get to the picnic table, he's not there, and neither are Patience and Zillah. The sleeping place Zillah made is empty, and part of the roof has fallen in—it's just a pile of sticks and rocks and plants now. Hallie pokes around in it, but doesn't find anything interesting.

"Stop that," says Adam. "Just leave it. He must've gone home."

"Do you think?" asks Dorcas, nervous.

"Sure." Adam seems relieved by Eddie's absence. "Patience and your sister are probably helping him get back across the wall."

Dorcas's forehead wrinkles. "I hope Zillah doesn't try and go with him."

"Stop talking about the demon," whines Sarah. "He went back to Hell. We don't have to think about him or his lies again." She starts marching back up the hill, Mary following close on her heels and Sharon trailing a little way behind. Hallie stays on her knees in the dirt, poking at a stick with another, bigger stick. Adam and Dorcas look into each other's eyes for a long time before turning away.

In the evening, before dinner, we are surprised when Father Joshua gathers all us kids together in his receiving room. Some of us have never been in here before, and are disappointed with how plain it is: wooden walls and metal folding chairs everywhere and a big leather chair for Father Joshua near the front. A picture of Jesus hangs behind him, just over his head. There are no windows.

Patience and Zillah are standing next to Father Joshua's chair, one on either side of him. The skin around Zillah's eyes is swollen and bruised purpleblack.

Patience's lower lip is split. Both of them have had their long hair shaved down to stubble, and they look naked and wrong without it.

"Children," says Father Joshua, folding his tattooed hands in front of his belly, "please, sit." So we do.

"You know why you've been called here," he continues. Our heads bob up and down in unison, as if pulled by strings. "You have helped and harbored a creature from beyond the wall. An emissary of Hell, posing as a man in need. You tried to keep his presence a secret from me, but God sees all, children, and the truth will come out." He pauses for a moment. "You knew that what you did was against the law of God and of this community, but I can believe it was motivated by innocent compassion, in most of you. The lion's share of the responsibility belongs to these women here, your sisters in Christ, Patience Palmer and Zillah Harlow, who brought the demon into our land and encouraged you to engage with him. They may have been bewitched by his good looks and silver tongue, but they are old enough to know better." He points to Zillah, then to Patience. "They have been chastised, and they will spend the next three days in fasting and penitence. But first, so that there may be no further confusion, they have something to say to all of you."

There's a long, tense silence. The metal chairs are hurting our butts. All our palms are sweaty. Finally, Patience steps forward.

"We did wrong," she says, without emotion. "There are no more human beings outside the wall. There is no more world. There's only desert, and dead sea, and Satan and his demons. The man you saw was a demon and a liar. Put him out of your heads."

"Zillah," says Father Joshua.

Zillah stands still, her mouth a mutinous, silent slit.

"Zillah!" He kicks her calf with one of his pointy-toed boots.

"We're sorry we led you astray," says Zillah, but somehow she manages to make it sound like she's saying I hate you, Father Joshua.

"And?" His voice is sour, lacking its usual resonance. Father Joshua, we realize, hates Zillah at least as much as she hates him.

"The man you saw was a demon and a liar. Everything he said was a lie."

"Good." Father Joshua smiles, but he doesn't mean it. We can tell. "Children, that demon was an emissary of hate, come to turn you against the will of the Lord, against the will of your parents, against *me*." He shows us his knuckle tattoo that says *hate*. Then he starts smothering that fist with his other hand, the one whose knuckles say *love*. "But our God is a God of love, children, and His law is merciful. I won't punish you for this. I ask only that you repent, and you never harbor a serpent-tongued stranger like this again. Never do it, or you will feel the wrath of God as well as His love!" The hands finish their battle, and the hate hand sags, defeated. "Do I make myself clear?"

We nod.

"Good. Now instead of supper, I want you all to stay right here in this room praying and reflecting for an hour. Just to make certain you understand the seriousness of your transgression." He looks down at us sadly. "Except for you, Dorcas. I expect much better than this from my future bride. I'd like you to come down the hall with me."

Dorcas rises from her seat and follows Father Joshua without a word, her face smooth and expressionless. But her hands shake a little in the folds of her skirt.

We split apart. Not a we, but individuals. Children off in our own heads—

Hallie fidgets and twists her fingers into puzzle knots. She tries to pray, but it just feels like she's using the voice in her head to shout out to nothing. God has to be real—right?—because everyone says He is, but Hallie's never been able to sense His presence. When Hallie looks at the world, there's nothing in it but world. When Hallie listens to the silence and stillness (or as close as she's ever going to get to silence, to stillness), she doesn't hear anybody except Hallie. Hallie talking to Hallie.

Hallie asks herself whether Zillah and Patience did anything wrong. Hallie answers that she doesn't think so.

Hallie asks herself whether Eddie was a demon, and Hallie answers that he wasn't. He was obviously a man. Hallie's always tried to trust her parents, and the Brothers, and Father Joshua. She wants to be good. She's tried really, really hard. But in the end, she can't help trusting herself more. Trusting the evidence of her own eyes and ears.

And Zillah? Hallie asks herself. Do I trust Zillah?

Yes, Hallie answers. She feels suddenly sure that Zillah has never knowingly lied to her, and that Father Joshua just has.

Adam sits as straight and stiff as a cross, his hands gripping his knees. He's trying to do a breathing trick Patience taught him for keeping calm. Three seconds in, hold for three seconds, three seconds out. He thinks it's starting to work. He thinks something terrible is happening to Dorcas. He thinks if he were a real man—if he were like David or Paul or Moses, if he were like the Brothers, if he were like his father (who is also Hallie's father and Mary's), if he were like Father Joshua, he would get up and run out of the room and down the hall. He would find Dorcas and grab her hand and run away with her. He knows they feel the same way about each other.

But Adam is weak, and he's stupid, and helpless, practically a child, and he doesn't want to be anything like Father Joshua, anyway. He doesn't want to treat girls like things to collect. He doesn't want to hit people or make other people do his hitting for him. He doesn't know what he does want, except Dorcas. And to be somewhere else.

Sharon is crying. She can't help it. She's trying at least to make it quiet crying, but that's not working. She gasps and hiccups and sniffles like she's three years old instead of thirteen. At first she thought she was crying from remorse for her sins. Then she realized, no. She's crying out of fear. Fear of God, fear of Hell, but mostly fear of Father Joshua.

Mary looks at the faded yellow dots on her skirt. She looks at the white flecks on her fingernails. She's soiled and speckled. She's a sinner. She's damned. She will grow up worse than Zillah, she's sure of it, unless God has mercy and makes her heart clean, expunges all the doubt, all the thoughts about Adam, about Eddie, about Jesus Himself, the way He looks in Father Joshua's tattoo and in paintings. *Forgive me,* she mouths silently, over and over. *Forgive me.*

Patience knows her mother will be emotional when she sees her daughter's shaved head and split lip. Maybe she'll be angry. Rage and spit and scream at Patience, tell her she should have died instead of little Isaac. If Patience had died and Isaac had lived, maybe Brother Ethan's other wife, Irene, would still speak to Patience's mother. Maybe Brother Ethan would still love them both.

Patience knows it's nonsense, of course. But knowing doesn't make it easier to endure her mother's screaming. Sometimes, in the thick of a tirade, Patience hates her mother. She wishes her mother were dead. She does feel guilty about that. Perhaps she is an awful daughter.

Zillah's crooked hand clasps hers. She squeezes gently. Zillah's earthy, familiar smell is in her nose. She doesn't even need to look over at her to take comfort. She doesn't want to see Zillah beaten and shorn, anyway.

It's not right that someone like Zillah can be hurt as easily as anyone else. It's dispiriting.

Maybe Patience's mother won't be angry after all. Maybe she'll be afraid. Maybe she won't recognize her daughter. That happens sometimes, when Patience wears her hair differently or gets new clothes. Maybe her mother will cower away from the strange, battered specter standing in her doorway, and Patience will have to soothe her calm again. *It's all right. It's only me. I'm here to take care of you.* She'll imagine Zillah with her as she gives her mother tonic and puts her to bed.

Zillah loves the feel of Patience's hands. They're callused, of course, but somehow soft and supple still in a way Zillah's aren't. They're pleasantly cool, with long fingers and broad palms. Zillah could hold Patience's hand all day. She thinks about that, about holding Patience's hand all day. She doesn't want to think about anything else right now. Later. Thinking comes later.

Dorcas feels like she's being split in two. Father Joshua's sweat falls on her face. He's not looking at her, but at something above and beyond her. God, maybe. Dorcas has given up on trying to enjoy the thing that's happening. She's not meant to enjoy it, anyway. She's meant to be put in her place.

*Maybe Father Joshua has the right,* Dorcas thinks, *but I can't stand this much longer.*

What will happen if she pushes him off, tries to squirm away? Her insides burn. It's like she's being prodded with a torch, again and again, fire scraping her body hollow. She tries to focus on the sensation of the wood floor beneath her back, how smooth and cool it is. She spreads her palms against it, wishing she could sink straight through.

Will this happen every night, once she's married? Every week? Every month? She can't do it. She *can't*. Dorcas isn't like her sister, she's never been brave. She's never had much ability to tolerate pain.

Father Joshua moans like a cow. Dorcas bites the inside of her cheek to keep from crying out.


Sarah stares steadily at the painting of Jesus. His eyes are blue, like Adam's, but flat and pitiless. He knows everything she's ever done, but that's okay. Sarah is righteous. She knows the difference between good and evil, and she always chooses good. Eventually, she always chooses good.

Sarah has never done anything really wrong. She's never caused any real harm, never made a mistake that couldn't be fixed. She's not like Zillah—she's not a ruiner. She's faithful. She follows rules. If she still feels guilty, what does that mean? She has nothing to feel guilty about. Only falling short of perfection, maybe, as all people inevitably do. Every man, woman, and child is a sinner from birth. That's what Jesus's gaze is communicating to Sarah. She has looked at Adam with his shirt off, she has pitied Zillah, she has felt fear and disgust when Father Joshua took Dorcas out of the room with him. She felt fear and disgust the way she'd felt fear and disgust for the demon, Eddie. Sarah is filled with fear and disgust, and some of it's misguided. Some of it's bad.

*Please, Lord God,* Sarah prays. *Help me make my feelings right. Help me do Your work in the world. Help me embody Your mercy and Your justice. Soak me in Your cleansing waters.*

*And if You don't see fit to do that, please give me what I deserve.*

Next morning there's meat at breakfast, mixed up with the egg scramble. It's surprising: we're nowhere near Easter, and Zillah hasn't caught anything big lately. The meat has a rich, oily, slightly bitter taste that's not like any meat we've had before. Some of us take a few bites and push the rest to the side of our plates. None of us think hard about where it came from. It's probably not a sin to eat a demon, no matter how human he looks. We don't know if it's a sin to eat a man or not.

Dorcas eats all of hers in a series of tiny, business-like bites. We were afraid she might return to us looking beat up like Zillah and Patience, but she's the same as ever. Only quieter, and sort of more careful in how she moves.

Sarah asks her about her time alone with Father Joshua, and she just looks straight ahead for several seconds with the blank face of a statue. Then she turns to Sarah and takes her hand and says, very low and serious, "You thought you were doing the right thing. I forgive you."

Sarah pulls away and makes a face. "For what?"

No answer.

There's meat at dinner, and there's meat the next day, too. It's the same meat, with the same strange taste, and then it's gone. Zillah spends more and more time out in the woods, but we don't have meat anymore. She says the animals are avoiding her traps.

Patience goes into the woods with her and they come back flushed and glittering, almost beautiful, with dirt under their fingernails and their baldness turning to bristle.

Dorcas cries when she thinks we're not looking and won't let Adam near her.

We don't meet at the picnic table so much. We try very hard to be good, throwing ourselves into our chores. Even Hallie is subdued, darning socks and helping tend the gardens, feeding the horses when Dorcas talks Father Joshua into letting her. She is solemn under Dorcas's watch, with the velvet nose of a horse nudging into the palm of her hand. We don't look at Adam when he takes off his shirt. We do our very best not to remember Eddie. We do our best not to daydream about a world that isn't here, and isn't dead.

Our best isn't enough. But it helps, a little. Autumn creeps closer. We settle into new routines.

Zillah's bruises have faded to a yellow that's hard to tell from her usual sallow complexion when she gathers us together at the picnic table for the last time.

Sarah and Mary don't come, but the rest of us do, even timid Sharon. Even Adam, though he seems restless and uncomfortable. We hope this means maybe things will go back to normal, but we all know it's something else.

Patience stands beside Zillah looking proud. Zillah is crackling with energy. The sky is low and gray above the forest, where a few trees have already begun to redden.

"You're all trustworthy," Zillah says. "But if any of you believe a single word Father Joshua has ever said, turn away now and go home. Read the Bible. Be obedient servants."

Dorcas's eyes brim with tears. Sharon gasps. Adam makes like he's going to walk away, but then he doesn't. None of us do.

"Fine," says Zillah. "Good." She takes something from her apron pocket and gives it to Hallie. "I found this in one of the compost piles. Cleaned it off. You can keep it, if you'd like."

Hallie cries out in wonder. It's Eddie's plastic and metal disc, only a little bit scratched. She presses every button on it, but it stays silent and doesn't show us any pictures. Still, her smile is wide as she transfers the thing to her own pocket.

"Thank you, Zillah. I'll keep it forever and ever. You know, we were going to get married."

"Yeah," says Zillah. She turns toward the treeline. "Everyone, follow me now."

We don't quite know why, but we obey. Even though it's just Zillah. She takes us over moss and through tangles of bramble, across streams and a meadow full of tall weeds and flowers. We see a white deer moving through the birches and maples ahead of us at one point, and when we get a little closer, we realize it doesn't have any eyes, just smooth skin stretched over its eye sockets. But it hears us coming, and it bounds off until it's lost in the peeling gray-white of birch trunks.

None of us have ever seen that deer before. Maybe it's a demon. Maybe it got in from outside, somehow. Maybe it just knows how to hide really well. We're far into the woods, must be almost to the wall.

And there it is. Tall, not rough enough to climb, not rough at all. How could Zillah have thought she might climb it, even for a second? It's smooth as glass, and shining. Rising above most of the trees.

There's a big pile of sticks and stones sitting at its base like a broken toy, lying on the bare dirt and trimmed down grass. Zillah moves the sticks and stones aside one by one, revealing a square of old tarp. She peels the tarp aside, and there are three warped wooden planks. She takes each plank in her arms and places it on top of the sticks and stones, and underneath the planks there is a deep dirt hole. It's so wide it's almost a cave. Just big enough to crawl through, if you're a kid or a small adult.

"It goes under the wall," says Zillah, like we hadn't figured that out already. "I've been through, once. There are trees out there, and vines, just like Eddie said. There are these ruined machines lying around, rusting. There's an old road that reaches way off into the distance."

"How'd you do it?" asks Adam. "How long have you—it must've taken ages."

"Months," agrees Zillah. "Patience helped. She brought the shovels."

"Mother never notices when things go missing for a while." Patience smiles, and Zillah smiles back. Their eyes are soft on each other's faces, and we realize there's something between them, something like what's between Adam and Dorcas. This is a possibility we've never considered before, that such things can come to exist between two girls.

"We finished yesterday," says Zillah. "We're going through in an hour."

"To give you enough time to go back and collect food, matches, canteens, any small thing you want to take," says Patience. "We want you all to join us."

"We're running away!" exclaims Hallie.

"What about our parents?" asks Sharon.

"Your parents will live without you." Zillah shrugs. "How often do any of you see your parents, anyway, apart from when you're waking up and going to bed? How often do you really think about them?"

"I'm supposed to get married," says Dorcas.

"You can't want to. Not after what he did." Zillah sounds angry.

"No, but... what if we're followed?"

"Father Joshua probably won't want to lose face and admit the world's alive on the other side, but it's a risk. I'll do my best to keep everyone safe."

Dorcas looks extremely doubtful.

"What if one of us tells, in the hour before you go through?" Adam asks. "How can you trust us?"

"I don't think you want to kill me or Patience," says Zillah. "And I know you know it would be killing us to tell. Maybe I'm a fool. Are you going to prove me a fool, Adam? Are you going to be a murderer?" She stares at him until he flushes and turns his face to the disrupted ground.

"Go," says Patience, kindly. "One hour. We won't

wait past that." She has an old gold-colored watch on her wrist from somewhere. Probably it was her mother's in the time before the wall. We can hear its hands go tick-tick-tick.

And we turn, and we go back into the woods. None of us run, not even Hallie, and none of us drag our feet. We walk with purpose. What that purpose is, we haven't yet decided.

The world within the wall is safe and known and it hasn't been so very unkind to any of us. Even Dorcas's pain is endurable. She could learn to endure it. It's not such a bad thing to be married to a powerful man and wear a pretty dress and have three sister wives to share duties with you, is it?

But beyond the wall, Dorcas maybe would never have to be a wife at all, unless she wanted to. Father Joshua would never stick his thing inside her. Beyond the wall, maybe people never eat each other. And there are cities full of buildings like crystal knives. And there are young men handsomer even than Adam. And maybe there are wastelands and demons. Maybe there's everything.

But Eddie had wanted to leave his home too. He wanted to run away to us. Maybe it's not different out there after all. Maybe it's the same thing over and over, all the way to the world's true edge. But Eddie's reasons for running were so stupid. Imagine, being bored because you didn't have to work hard. Our lives are lived in the gaps between hard work. You can't think well when you're bent over rows of seedlings in the hot sun, scrubbing dishes, churning butter, digging a latrine. For hours and hours, with rationed water and not always enough to eat.

But who says we won't still have to do those things outside?

But maybe it will be different if we're doing them just because we want to. If we don't have to answer to anybody but ourselves.

But maybe it's all a trick and a lie. Maybe we will come back and there will be a pair of demons by the hole instead of Zillah and Patience, two demons with their long hairy tails intertwined. Maybe we will come back and Patience and Zillah will be gone, and the hole will be gone, too. Maybe, maybe, maybe. But, if.

Our brains keep turning in circles as our feet keep stepping forward through the birches and maples and oaks. Soon, we'll each have to make a decision. Soon, we'll see the picnic table peeking at us between the trees, and then we'll be under the open sky, and then we'll see the whole compound stretched out before us from the top of the hill.

# About the Author

Briar Ripley Page is also the author of *Body After Body*, *The False Sister*, and *Travelers' Tales* (a chapbook collection of stories). Briar currently lives in London with their partner and two black-and-white cats. In addition to writing, Briar has been a janitor, a hotel maid, a dishwasher, a waiter, a receptionist, an illustrator, a sandwich artist, a day camp supervisor, a dogsitter, and a full time crazy person. They like glass, fire, worms, forests, and the sea. Find Briar online at briarripleypage.xyz and flameswallower.itch.io.

# About the Press

tRaum Books is a tiny press dedicated to seeking out works that play with, quietly challenge, or aggressively fuck with binaries and norms, especially regarding gender and sexuality. Based in Munich, Germany, we are happy and proud to work with talented authors from all over the world. If you'd like to see more of our books, please visit us at www.traumbooks.com.

A special thank you to the following people, for making our projects possible.

Dermitzel
Brak
Jun Nozaki
Leon Sorensen
Clacks
Agnes Merey
Gele Croom
Philip O'Loughlin
Steven Askew
Tucker Lieberman
Lachelle Seville
Anna Otto

www.ingramcontent.com/pod-product-compliance
Lightning Source LLC
LaVergne TN
LVHW041451230325
806627LV00030B/756